SORROWS

JONATHAN CREED
BOOK 2

JOHN A. CURLEY

ROUGH
EDGES
PRESS

Rough Edges Press
An Imprint of Wolfpack Publishing
9850 S. Maryland Parkway, Suite A-5 #323
Las Vegas, Nevada 89183

roughedgespress.com

Paperback ISBN 978-1-68549-215-1
eBook ISBN 978-1-68549-214-4
LCCN 2022948932

DEDICATION

This book is dedicated to Andrew Vachss. There will never be another like him. I have been fortunate in my life in that I have frequently worked and interacted with some of the best and brightest people there are. Andrew was, in fact, the most intelligent, logical, and disciplined person I have ever known. I frequently fail at making people understand just how smart and strong he was. He directed that logical intelligence, combined it with his cold hatred of predators, and dedicated his life to child protection. He would often say he made no secret of the fact he dedicated his life to child protection because of his hatred of predators, not because of his love for children. But once you got to know him, there was no denying his love for children, our children, was there. He was apolitical, knowing both sides of the aisle consistently fail children and often make it worse.

I have no idea what he saw in me that made me worth so much of his time. He was my mentor in both writing and child protection. He was my friend and father figure, which I had thought was due to my age when we started interacting and not something I'd experience again. I learned every time we spoke. He never asked me for anything. I did know he wanted people to continue his work, his message. I'm not him, no one could be. But I promised him early on that his fight was mine for as long as I was here. I do not "take into account" what Andrew knew. I do not "re-interpret" it. It would be like drawing a mustache on the Mona Lisa or putting a footnote on the General Relativity. His principles, his understanding of predators, and his knowledge cannot be improved upon by me. Point of fact is, they can't be improved upon—period.

I grew to love Andrew, but the idea that he was Andrew Vachss never left me. I followed his lead, not because I loved him, but because 35 years of watching the system fail children consistently and seeing his points about where it can be improved upon match up perfectly. Familiarity did not breed contempt. I would ask questions, and he would patiently answer. I took for granted that if we disagreed on a subject, he was most likely right. He took that intellect, logic, and discipline that was so formidable and brought war to those who prey on children. Although I had the advantage and privilege of his friendship, everything he taught me is available to anyone that wants that knowledge. Just visit Vachss.com.

I would never say "Rest in Peace." Andrew lived to fight. If there is a way, he is still fighting. We had plans to do things we did not get to complete. But I took notes, and I will see it through to the end. Because he contracted malaria in Biafra, we were never able to have that drink. But I hedged my bets there. I spoke with him when I was making a donation to the Legislative Drafting Institute for Child Protection. I told him I'd be happy to double it (no cigars that month then). If he arrived at Valhalla first, he would not drink, but wait for me to arrive. And I would be the first person he would drink with that way. He agreed. I'm sure he is still the most patient and disciplined person I've ever known.

As he is likely reading this: I will see you soon enough pal. I miss the hell out of talking with you, and I thank you for everything. I also miss that sense of humor most people didn't realize you had. I love you, Papa V. See you when I get there.

I also dedicate this book to Alice Vachss. We all lost him, but you lost a husband. He told me on more than one occasion you were every bit the warrior he was and then some. Thank you for your advice and encouragement.

SORROWS

PROLOGUE

IF YOU WERE WATCHING me as I tried to get into the back door of my office, you'd have thought I was drunk or breaking in. I was unsteady on my feet and at one point, I leaned my head up against the door. It was metal and it was cold and it felt good. I must have scratched the hell out of the door as I missed the keyhole at least a dozen times.

Eventually I got the key in, entered the wrong number in the alarm box enough times that after I finally got it right the phone rang.

"Hi, code is Burke. I'm sorry, I'm tired," I told the girl verifying who I was. My voice was slow and slurred but that was because my mouth was swollen and not because of booze. Hopefully that would change in a bit. I stumbled into my office without locking the door.

Squinting when I flicked the light switch on didn't make my face feel any better. I looked at myself in the mirror over the bar. There was not, I think, one square inch of my body that wasn't in pain. My nose was broken but I could breathe okay and it was broken straight. My mouth was swollen, my left eye almost closed and a nice cut over my right eye. Painful as it was, I felt my shoulder, the one where I had the surgery after I was shot. It didn't feel like I had screwed up the repair. When I moved my fingers to my ribs that caused me to exhale and cough. And by cough I mean a near death experience. I opened the little fridge and got the ice pack I kept in the tiny freezer out and I grabbed the Jamieson bottle and sat behind my desk. No, I dropped into the chair. Part voluntarily and partly because my legs gave out. The pain in my left knee and right ankle decided they were not getting equal attention. I might have a concussion too. I opened the desk draw. There was oxycodone, aspirin, some muscle relaxants, and Advil. I got the bottles of oxy and the muscle relaxant—flexorsomething or other—open and took two of each and four aspirin. When I dropped the bottles back into the drawer all the pills fell out and made a really pretty pattern. I took a deep swallow and, damn, the fucking burn from the cut in my mouth coming into contact with the whiskey. Sorry, it called for the vulgarity.

"Work through the pain, Jimmy Boy," I said to myself. I swallowed some more; I'm guessing the equivalent of two double shots so far.

"Okay let's not kill ourselves," I thought.

"Why the fuck not?" I answered aloud.

I took another pull, but it was just a sip. I swished it around felt the burn intensify. I put the bottle on the desk, and it fell over. It didn't matter. There was only about a teaspoon left. Time to head to the pharmacy.

Everything hurt. I looked at my knuckles, took a second to focus on them. There was a cut on my left hand, and both hands were bruised and swollen. That took a lot. I wondered if he was dead. Probably not, but I didn't care. That'd be something, though. I'd have killed two guys with my bare hands. My ribs vociferously protested when I leaned back in the chair. I felt them again. I didn't think they were broken but who the hell knows?

Sleep started to force its way in, the adrenaline gone. I was exhausted. Leaning back had been a mistake, and it turns out so was putting my head on the desk. I pushed back a little, found the wall and a position sort of leaning back, but not as far and closed my eyes, pressing the cold pack against my face. Holding it there till the wall clock said fifteen minutes had passed while fighting off sleep was perhaps the greatest feat of willpower I had ever accomplished. I thought about Mandy, Vicki, and then Cory. And then Rain. My eyes welled up and some tears flowed but not a lot. At some point I dropped the cold pack and fell asleep.

PART I

Just around the corner
a distant shadow
fleeing.

I try to catch up
always out of breath
muscles aching, cramping
eyes bleary, mind dizzy
trying to answer why.

Ignoring how
and just accepting
the what of is.

The Time Traveler
Charles H. Johnson

1

New Year's Eve. The stores would be closing about seven. I had gone to a craft store called Michael's. I was going to pick up a gift card for my friend's daughter, a belated Christmas present as she had apparently inherited some of her father's artistic abilities. When I suggested a gift from the crafts store he had told me a gift card would be great. When I had asked what his other daughter might want he told me a gift card from a place called Gamestop would work. I lucked out. Apparently Michael's also carried gift cards for Gamestop. Not that I had anywhere to go but I was fairly certain I wouldn't enjoy being in a place called Gamestop. The young Indian or Pakistani girl that cheerfully rang me up reminded me of a woman I had known and spent time with, although she was very young. When she smiled at me I smiled back and wished her a happy New Year. I had secured the gifts I would bring for the New Year's day dinner I had been invited to. I had secured a case of excellent Merlo and would give a bottle to my friend and his wife.

Although I was not hungry I decided to go to the supermarket to pick up a few things. The guys tailing me were sloppy and I had figured it out a while back. They were using two cars, a big guy with a pea coat, and either a smaller guy or a woman. A black Dodge Charger and of all things a PT cruiser. Pea coat drove the cruiser.

I picked up a few things in Shoprite and as in Michael's, they didn't follow me in. The lines were long. I got on the express line, 12 items or less. I had 14 items. As I stood online I wondered if the supermarket police might come and remove me. The line advanced and the old black woman in front of me who had a jar of herring and nothing else in the cart put the bottled fish on the conveyer. The kid was helping her run a food stamp card through. It was taking some time. There was grumbling behind me. I didn't care, I was in no rush. A man and a woman a couple of lines over argued loudly. The Doppler effect kind of kicked in as she yelled back at him as she walked away, and he remained in line. I determined from the exchange she had walked into him. Tis the season. The woman in front with the food stamp card was 83 cents short on the card. She asked the kid if he could hold her bottled fish while she went to her car and got money. I gave the kid the dollar. The woman turned toward me with arthritic slowness and smiled and thanked me. I smiled back and told her it was my pleasure. I noticed she had trouble walking and appeared to use the cart to help her walk. The kid asked me if I had any coupons, and I replied no and he rang up my items. I gave him the fake phone number I had used when I applied for the supermarket discount card. I paid for my goods and wished him a happy New Year even though he didn't remind me of anyone I had slept with.

I walked to the cigar store a few store fronts away from the supermarket, and aside from wanting a few, used that as an opportunity to see what the Peacoat and the ambiguous gender partner were doing. No apparent ambush planned. Peacoat of the PT was in his cruiser a few aisles away from me. I passed the black Charger which had unfortunately parked near the cigar store with its occupant in it. I still couldn't tell for sure if it was a woman. The Charger had Jersey plates. As I got close I saw it was a girl, and at first glance she appeared to be cute but alas I couldn't tell if she reminded me of anyone I had slept with. She was young. She became fidgety, uncomfortable; I imagined because I was close to her. I went in and picked out a few cigars, including the 50 dollar La Diva cigar the owner had in his back room. La Divas were no longer made but he had a few boxes. They were almost Churchill sized but torpedo shaped and had been infused with a very fine cognac. I knew they weren't government or cops. I hadn't pissed off any wise-guys I knew of recently, and not to be sexist, but the boys usually didn't use a female surveillance op. In that case they followed you briefly, delivered their message either with words, fists, or bullets, and moved on. Amateurs. It was New Year's Eve; somebody may not have been able to be too choosy about who they got to do a tail job. They could be from anywhere but I'm sure if I thought about it I could narrow the list down. They could be rental cars but probably not. The Cruiser had New York plates and as I had seen the Charger had Joisey plates. I smiled to myself and I pronounced it in my mind like I was from Nu Yawk. As I often told clients, never let on you know you are being tailed. I didn't want them tailing me to the cemetery but I didn't want them to know I knew, either. I had the Charger plate and as I walked toward my car I got the Cruiser plate. I wrote them down when I got in my car.

There was the list as I often jokingly referred to it. There was more than one person walking around and a few sitting in jail cells who would have their days brighten considerably if they learned of say an unfortunate (or fortunate depending on the perspective) demise on my part. Not all pi's garnered that kind of following but I, ever the patron saint of lost causes and wielder of the sword to fight perceived miscarriages of justice, had indeed managed to piss a few people off here and there. I also managed to get the woman I loved killed.

As I did not, however, want them following me to the cemetery and I needed to go there, the key thing was to lose them in such a way that even an amateur would chalk it up to happenstance. Most inexperienced people thought every time the subject looked in their direction, they got made. In truth I had actually thrown them a few bones and they were having trouble staying with me. As I pulled out of the parking lot three or four cars pulled out after me. Peacoat was nowhere to be seen and Charger girl jockeyed for position to catch up and was thwarted by, I think, the old woman from the market. I smiled as I got on the highway.

"Now, that is paying it forward. Best 83 cents I ever spent."

When I got on what was now called the Martin Luther King Jr. Expressway but (no disrespect to Dr. King) was always going to be the Staten Island Expressway, I sped up to highway speed. Charger girl was four cars back; all four of the cars, by the way, were cutting over to get on the expressway so she was stuck. In a few seconds, due to the slight elevation of the road, I was out of view and hit the gas heavier. The expressway split up into three directions. To the far left it ended on Victory Blvd. In the middle it turned onto the Staten Island Expressway going east toward the Verrazano Bridge. To the far right it turned onto the Staten Island Expressway going west to the Goethals Bridge and West Shore Expressway. I took that route, came onto the Staten Island Expressway, and took the first exit which put me onto Richmond Ave. I went North on Richmond, passed the supermarket and cigar store I had been to, and Richmond turned onto Morningstar Rd. I made a right at the Terrace and took the streets to the cemetery. The sign said closed after dusk.

I knew there was no guard. A lot of my family rested there. It was situated between a park and a zoo. Sometimes on warmer nights in spring, summer, and fall you could hear as you were walking by or stopped at a traffic light the sounds of some of the animals. I didn't go there too often but often enough to stop by and see them. I was alone and I had turned the car lights off. No one would likely realize I was there. I took a short cigar that I had gotten at the shop and used a cigar lighter that had a hole punch in the bottom to light it. If my only goal was invisibility I wouldn't have done it, of course, but like many things, I didn't really care. I said hello and happy holidays to all, knowing the way well enough in the dark. I lastly stopped at her grave. She actually never really minded my cigars. I talked to her for a while. It was not a scary place to me; it was more a place of tribute and of remembrance. I had for months come here on a semi-daily basis. I talked with her often though it didn't have to be in the cemetery. I stood there for a while. It was a short cigar and in about 20 minutes the foot was close enough that I could feel the heat on my lips. I flicked the ash once more, crushed the end on the pavement as I walked back to the car, and out of respect, I took the remains of the cigar and put it in the empty coffee cup. I took an antique flask out of the glove compartment that I had bought with her and raised it in a symbolic gesture to all and swallowed some Jamieson. I wasn't concerned that a single swallow would put my two hundred and forty plus pound frame in the DUI realm.

I drove home and there was Peacoat and Charger Girl. Peacoat was parked almost directly in front of my house. Idiot. Charger Girl was down the street about as far as she could be and still see the house. I had to suppress laughter as Peacoat, trying not to be noticed, was actually holding a newspaper in front of him... Too many things wrong with that to list.

For Peacoat's benefit I went to my trunk while carrying the small bag I got from the supermarket and took out some stuff I had picked up a few days earlier at Best Buy. It would ease his mind thinking that I had gone to Best Buy when they lost me. Provided he was alert enough to notice the bag. I had been considering who may have sent them and I had narrowed it down to a few, taking into account the amateurish nature. It could have been another PI who got a last-minute job in on a holiday that was desperate for help. I had been in that position myself a few times. Or it was someone who was just using amateurs for whatever reason, maybe money maybe not. It was likely related to a case. I wasn't currently dating any married women and hadn't pissed anyone off too badly lately except a few people on cases that I was working against. I had a pretty good idea. I'd likely know for sure once I got inside.

"All I want is a room somewhere far away from the cold night air," I sang softly to myself as I went to the side of the house, deactivated the fortress, and went in.

There was a cat that lived in the basement now, a rescue who had come up to me holding his paw off the ground crying. I took him to the vet, they fixed him up, and he adopted me. I rarely saw him but when I did he tolerated me. Once in a while, he had the knack of throwing up on one of my forty-five-pound plates, and a lot of googling left me with no explanation.

There was Molly, upstairs sleeping in the kitchen, who had been a rescue earlier in the year from SICAW (or for those not in the know, the Staten Island Council for Animal Welfare). My friend Cheryl at the vet's office had stopped by to see how I was doing and remarked that they had some of SICAW's dogs that were for adoption at her office. She had said they were afraid no one was going to take Molly. She hid in her cage and was quiet all the time. I had said I'd think about it and she brought Molly the next day. She told me they were hoping I could foster her. I smiled and said fine. Molly hid at first and then slowly made her way to me. Cheryl sat with us a while. I was quiet. I started to apologize for being so quiet and she hushed me and sat with me and held my hand a while. After a half hour, Molly sat on the couch with her head on my lap. Cheryl got up and kissed me gently, kissed Molly on top of her head, and she left.

She was a mutt, small, less than 25 pounds, and had

one blue eye and one brown eye. When I came in I heard the tail thumping before I got in the kitchen through the door that connected the basement, the kitchen, and the heavily used side door. She didn't mind my singing. I put the bags down, said hi to Molly, and put the groceries away.

It was already 8pm. I flipped the Christmas lights on and put some music on. Carol Miller was working. I looked across the room and saw her picture. It had been a while, but sometimes like now, I misted a little, but that was all. I had lost people before but I had no idea how deeply sorrow could go. My brothers had asked me to come over and I had received a few other invites as well, but I was staying in tonight. The most noticeable fact about the coming year is I would not be spending it with her. I enjoyed cooking and sometimes liked to cook for myself even if I was alone, but I didn't feel like it. I had worked too hard coming back and I hadn't eaten, so I went into the kitchen and threw some stuff in a blender—almond milk, peanut butter, a couple of apples, some greens I had, a carrot, some blueberries, and protein powder. I brought that into the living room. Molly followed me and jumped on the couch next to me and laid her head in my lap. I drank supper and stared at her picture. I was trying to decide what to do with the rest of the night. I had been rereading a book by Carl Sagan, and a new PI novel I had been wanting to read had come out, but I didn't feel like that, either. I put the TV on, looked at the guide, and saw a lot of things that would normally interest me. But they didn't at the moment. I didn't feel like drinking and not at all like scaring up a date. I made the music a little softer. There were far worse ways to spend time than with Carol

Miller, Pink Floyd, and my dog. I got out my laptop and plugged into a database I subscribed to.

A few minutes later I knew Peacoat was Bruno Tagliano and Dodge Charger was Danielle Gennaro, he 38 and she 29. He was a licensed realtor. I looked further into them. She was a neighbor at one time to Diane Cretella. Bruno was employed by the same real estate firm that was selling Diane's house. It was one of the nastier divorce cases I was working on, and as a matter of fact, it was one of the worst I'd ever worked on.

I was thinking it was her from the start and was happy my intuition still worked. I toyed with the idea of going outside and wishing Bruno a Happy New Year by name just to see the expression on his face, but I knew I wasn't going to do that. They both had Facebook accounts. My eyes rolled back a little involuntarily as his profile had a shirtless picture. One of the pages he liked was Ragin (not Raging) Bull. One of his other pictures had him wearing a turtle neck and a sports jacket with a gold cross on the outside of the turtleneck. That made me wince. Having some Italian blood in me myself— with the cooking ability and the chest hair to prove it—I found the Jersey Shore segment of the population, although less painful than appendicitis, more irritating than say, a boil on the ass. He also made reference on several posts about doing "PI" work.

Danielle on the other hand was quite pretty, and as I read her posts and comments she seemed to be a sweet kid. They were both typical of Diane's recruits. She likely had been told a story far different from reality and I'm sure there were a lot of tears involved and pleas for help. It turned out she was a SICAW member. That could be helpful later on. Bruno's friends apparently called him "Truck." Truck (I liked "Peacoat" better) had most likely heard the song of the mentally unbalanced siren. Maybe at some point he'd find out she'd had warts. She had blamed that on her husband, my client also, early on in the court proceeding. My client had gone for tests and it turns out he did not have the virus. I wondered what Peacoat would have to say about that.

Her custody case was going badly; this was likely desperation. Following the other side's PI was desperate. I had testified a few times already. Typical bullshit on this court case. If it was reversed, if my client was the mother, the father would be restricted to supervised visits once a week. Diane had three days one week and two days the following week and that repeated. The honest to God truth, going by my experience, was the mother was most often more suited, especially for younger children. But not always. Every custody or abuse case that was not judged solely on its own merits and facts ended up hurting the kids. The judge couldn't get past taking custody from the mother. Forcing him to was not easy or expeditious.

My testimony had been part of the reason she lost fifty-fifty custody. I guess if they found something bad, Diane figured it might help. Maybe she thought about bribing me.

I thought about calling my client; he was one of the invites I had turned down for tonight. I thought about calling his lawyer. She was one of the other invites I had turned down. I suddenly felt tired and old. The barrage of questions I'd get from the client would make my mood grow even worse and I didn't want to bother Rita, although she would find it interesting.

"Well, Miss," I said to Molly. "What shall we do?" Molly sighed.

I missed her most at times like this. I felt the emptiness inside. It is interesting to me, the parallels of emotional and physical injury. Not to mention going through them at the same time. The initial loss is a searing pain that eventually scales down to a dull, ever present ache, that would still on occasion flare back up to searing pain. It never left me entirely. I didn't think it ever would.

None of us are a stranger to loss. Depending on who you were and where you were in your life and a variety of other factors, we all experienced it. Some more than others. Now I was in the "some" category. Sometimes I'd think of her and my heart would race and I'd feel the panic that came with the certainty she was gone. I got up carefully as not to overly disturb Molly and grabbed a bottle of Jamieson from the bar. I returned to the couch and basically sat there and thought and sipped whiskey. The thought of another cigar came and went. That's what I did until Molly and I went to bed.

I stopped in the bathroom and took off my shirt. I washed my bearded face; it had grown in when I couldn't shave for eleven weeks. The work on my shoulder had been extensive. I couldn't use it for the three months, so it would heal right. I kept conditioner on the bathroom sink for the beard. If you wanted to be clean you had to wash it twice a day, but that took the moisture off and it would be rough and bristly. It irritated me and no one else. There hadn't been anyone else. Strangely I didn't care if there was. That would probably pass. I knew that there would never be anyone like her.

I wasn't tired so we kept listening to the radio, but I had no more whiskey. Molly curled up at the foot of the bed in her usual spot and then went to sleep.

Eventually I slept, uneasily. After he shot her I had broken his neck. I held her while she died. Her blood was on me. I had brushed her hair back with my left hand while she was talking to me about her son, and I told her she would be okay. She was coughing but she smiled at me. I told her it would be okay, she would be okay, it would all be okay...the ambulance was coming. She said she was okay and smiled at me. The light went out of her eyes with the smile on her face. I looked at her a while.

The bullet which had gone through her and then through me had made a hole in the wall behind me. I had turned to look at it. I had no fucking idea why. I could hear sirens. And I heard the gurgling sound. I walked over and looked down at him. I didn't need to see his head at the weird angle to know his neck was broken. His eyes fixed on me. He was trying unsuccessfully to breathe. Tears were streaming down my face and the pain which had just started to set in gave way to rage. I kicked him as hard as I could in his head. His body was actually lifted and pushed away a few feet. The impact jarred my leg and knee and I thought I might have broken something in my foot. I didn't care. The gurgling stopped. That's what happened. That's what I dreamed almost every night.

When they had started to put me under anesthesia, I was hoping I wouldn't wake up. Another wish unfulfilled.

The last few months were a bit of a blur. Physical therapy, and copious amounts of physical pain dwarfed by a broken heart. First Vicki and then Mandy. I replayed everything over and over. I could have done things differently. I should have been better prepared. Mentally and emotionally I was numb for a while. To this day I would realize I'd never see her again and my heart would race and I would be near collapse. If only I had moved faster. If only I had checked the apartment. It was like reading a Wayne Dundee novel. Everything worked out for the best. Mission accomplished, and then when you started to breathe easy, someone died, right at the end.

I used the pain meds they gave me, but sometimes I chose not to because I found that searing physical pain actually garnered my attention and sometimes stopped me from thinking about Mandy dying as I held her. When I did think of her I often remembered killing Stanton. But all that just delayed the inevitable. In the past few weeks I'd wake up crying or I wouldn't make it into work on occasion, despite having not missed a day after I recovered from surgery. No matter how I looked at it, I couldn't get past that it was my fault. I forced myself to exercise. Molly was a big help. Friends and family were there for me. But her loss was always in the front of my thoughts. If she wasn't Vicki was, and thinking about Vicki would lead me back to Mandy.

Sleep took a while but eventually found its way to me. I woke several times and as usual dreamt about Mandy. And killing Stanton.

2

I GOT UP EARLY On New Year's Day. My shoulder was talking to me. After the three months I went for physical therapy, it turned out I had frozen shoulder. Everything had locked, and while I was going for PT I couldn't put my hand in my back pocket to get my wallet. The doctor had felt at the time it might happen.

"It often ends up that very heavily muscled people get it. Physical therapy should take care of it."

"If not?" I asked.

"Surgical procedure called manipulation under anesthesia. No cutting but we call it surgery because you are under and we basically beat the hell out of your shoulder."

I brewed strong coffee on the stove top, which is the best way to make it, and I let Molly out. The PT helped but not enough. They did the manipulation in September, after Labor Day. I had the use of my arm back, and the therapist gave me permission to start working out on my own. I was now able to hit the bag, and the strength came back slowly but it came back. I was at 60 percent and moving up slowly. It hadn't been arthroscopic. They opened my up and worked on me for three hours. The doctor told me that the years of strength training paid off.

"You don't have tendons, you have steel cables. You'll come back from this," the doctor had told me. before surgery. "This surgery is the most invasive but it is best for this type of wound. The recovery is longer but you'll be back to normal when it's done." I had chosen him because if I was forced to stick around this rock, I wanted to be me. He had operated on a number of athletes who were able to resume their careers, and as I was active, I wanted him. At one point he started telling me about the difficulties and I stopped him.

"Doc, I need the surgery, right?"

"Unless your tendon spontaneously reattaches itself, and if you want to raise your arm over your head again, yes."

"Then we will deal with what happens when it happens. Let's just get to it," I said.

I started stretching lightly and did some warm up calisthenics, ending with 30 push-ups and a hundred leg raises, pausing at one point to let the Molly in. She drank water and ate a cookie I tossed to her and then, apparently tired from the effort, went back to sleep.

I still required pain pills. Last month I'd only used them twenty out of thirty days. The shoulder hurt. You could, if you were sitting in the room when I did push-ups, hear the scar tissue pop. I wasn't afraid of addiction; that's not in my makeup. I do not dismiss the pain of others, but for me it wasn't a problem. I'll leave this earth addicted to Peter Luger steak, Breyers Ice Cream, and the occasional kinky sex thing. It was the searing pain in my shoulder which was quite impressive. I honestly didn't know you could feel that much physical pain prior. It was brutal, but it took my concentration off the emotional pain and the loss for stretches of time. The only side effect I thought was that they made me more emotional. I couldn't see things like the beach on television without thinking I'd not have the chance to take her someplace like that. But I didn't know for sure. I'd never gotten the woman I loved killed before.

I would see Shane every so often. Sometimes I would meet him after his class at Smitty's school and take him to eat and then home. He and his dad came over for dinner once and they had me over twice.

"I remember when snap, crackle, and pop, were the sounds my breakfast cereal made and not what I heard getting out of a chair or doing push-ups," I told the Physical Therapist. He worked his ass off with me. Mark Pacciano. I'd not forget him. I chose him because he had a doctorate in Physical Therapy. And he cared. The surgeon said there was less to do with the manipulation because Mark had worked so hard. Well, *we* worked so hard. I smiled as I remembered telling him how much I missed putting my arm behind my head.

"That's what we'll work on today!" he chirped with far too much enthusiasm. I have never loved and hated someone at the same time as much as him. I was surprised people across the Bridge didn't hear me scream that day. But I had gotten my arm behind my head.

I went down in to the basement and spent ten minutes or so punching the heavy bag—not full out with my right—and then rested and had my coffee. It was a medium day. I was a good month away from a heavy workout, and even then not what I was doing before. Not yet. I felt up to it. Squats, benches curls, and a little extra support work. I was doing a 5x5 work out. The last set on the squats had four plates on it. I felt pain in the shoulder but I breezed through the set. I still felt that twinge in the shoulder where the fragment of the bullet had gone through and that had prevented me from going much heavier.

I had also lucked out with Doctor Bhatia and his nurse, Kathleen. They did pain management. While there were people dying from overdoses, it's always a pendulum swing. Not long ago people were dying from end of life cancer pain and they couldn't get pain meds. Now it went the other way and doctors had given it out for hangnails. Mariano spent a lot of his time telling parents their son or daughter had overdosed in the basement. When I took them they were an effective tool. If it was the right dose, there was no euphoric feeling, it just cancelled out the pain. Most of the people that ended up having problems had taken them to get high in the first place or took them incorrectly. If you waited too long to take them, and the pain got bad, one pill wouldn't do it. I always took myself off for 4 or 5 days out of the month. I timed it so it was when the workouts were very light. That actually worried them a bit.

"On the one hand most addicts can't voluntarily go a week without on purpose, so it shows you don't have a problem, but you may have it so the pain runs away."

"So what am I doing wrong?"

"Let me guess...you wait until its unbearable most of the time before you take it?"

"Yeah."

"Jimmy, you have to get ahead of it. Take the meds

when you're supposed to. You're not suffering from side effects. We can transition later." I nodded in agreement, leaving out the part about using the physical pain as a band aid for my loss.

On the bench I did 245, my weight, as the last set. I shook a little on that set. I had been putting up close to four before I was shot. I had that goal for June. Go up five pounds a week. Thirty-one weeks. I finished with the supporting and grip work and then the hated treadmill. I walked for a half hour. I never had any knee problems and I was trying to keep it that way. I never ran the same days I did heavy squats. I had fractured a bone in my foot when I completed the break in Stanton's neck with it. That talked to me a little, then I was off the treadmill and stretched again.

Years ago I had read in the paper that a gym was going out of business and I got all professional equipment for the basement for a song. Over a thousand pounds of weight, a safety cage, dumbbells, and boxing and martial arts equipment.

After the therapy ended I took over. Slowly but steady I was getting back. I had the strength to do more but I was taking my time. Mark and the doctor, or Boris the Doctor's PA still checked on me once in a while. Ken Testa kept an eye on me also. I still had to go to pain management monthly because that was the law in New York. My state loves to get between a doctor and their patient. I smiled again.

Doctor Shur's staff had tried a couple of cortisone shots prior to the manipulation. It wasn't fun. It sort of worked for a day and then nothing.

"I can try one more. It may work, and if it does, no manipulation needed," he said and then paused.

I had smiled. "And?"

"This will hurt," he said. His accent as thick as it was it sounded like *hort*.

"Where you from, Doc?"

"Siberia."

"So pain to you is not like pain to me, right? What, did you only eat snow till you were twelve and you sliced off chunks of milk?"

We all laughed at that. "No, John, this will be painful, even by my standards. It may work, it may not. You decide. I'm going in the other way, right where I did the work. Huge nerves there. It will hurt."

I thought about it. I smiled again. "Fuck you, Doc," I said and winked.

He laughed. "Good! That's my man."

To say that it hurt was like saying the Sahara was a little dry. I asked him what he was going to do with the ginormous needle he brought out. He said it goes in.

"No, that's what you use to inseminate a horse," I said.

We laughed again. I didn't laugh when the needle went in. That was the most physically painful three seconds of my life. I sweated through my clothes in a second and it looked like I had jumped in a pool. The memory of it actually made me shiver.

It didn't work.

The day of the manipulation came. I got to the city early, at about five. I was in a cab and my phone rang. Some years back I met and become friends with Patrick Kilpatrick. He had been the bad guy in more movies than you could count. I had done a job for him and we became close after. A genuinely sweet guy, which made him playing parts where he got kicked into a furnace and came out on fire, still trying to kill the good guy, more bewildering. To go from being him in real life to a psycho like that, and to be believable, that was acting.

"Hey, Jimmy!" I was greeted with as I answered the phone. "Are you in the hospital yet?"

"Just got here, Sandman. Are you up super early or..."

"Haven't been to bed yet. I sent you a copy of my new book to read whilst you coalesce."

"What's the title?"

"*Dying For Living.*"

"Great title!"

"And I have important advice for you."

"Do tell, Sandman."

"Flirt with the nurses, this way they will have a vested interest in you coming out of it."

People in the lobby looked up as I entered the hospital laughing. I was met by a nurse and she took me to Doctor Shur. He was awake and alert like it was late morning. As I slipped into unconsciousness I had a smile on my face as I heard him saying "Okay, Jimmy, I'm gonna fix you now, you stubborn bastard."

As soon as I woke I could feel the difference. I was in bed and my right arm was tied to the frame above me. The Doc came right over.

"Now, you big pain in the ass, let's see my work and get you out of here. You're fixed."

He undid the knot and very gently lowered my arm to my chest. It was free. The drag of the scar tissue was gone. He almost punched me then because he asked me to move it. I pretended I couldn't and shook my head.

He actually yelled out, "No!"

And I said, "Just kidding."

There were a lot of bad memories. I missed Mandy every second of every minute of every hour of ever goddamned day. But the Doc and his crew, Doc Pacciano and his group Core Physical Therapy, and Dr. Bhatia and Kathleen from Richmond Pain Management, my friend Doc Testa were keeping an eye on me. It sometimes took me aback, that these people who all helped me get my arm back, lived to help people like me.

I rarely had breakfast for breakfast. But I did today. I put the oven on and took out the bacon, eggs, a couple of apples, and a loaf of Italian bread from the freezer. I lined a huge cast iron frying pan with bacon and put that on a low flame. It'd take a half hour to cook. I put the Italian bread into the oven at 200. I scrambled half dozen eggs. I had gone to Boston Market the other night and I took out the creamed spinach, red potatoes, and mixed vegetables. I went upstairs and took a quick shower. The aroma of the bacon met me as I got dressed. When I went down, I took the small loaf of warm bread out of the oven and put butter on it and it melted the way I liked. I went into the living room with the food, Molly awake now and in tow. I had made her a little bacon and eggs and put them on a plate for her next to the coffee table where I ate. I put the TV on and watched the news a bit. I saw the weather and felt the usual nausea when the hosts of the morning show pretended to talk about news. I often wondered how far back we would have to go to get actual news. How far back to where the news was reported and the viewer decided what it meant. The current occupant of the White House had made a comment about someone. The reporter of the local station was clearly enraged.

The reporter on the conservative station didn't think it was a big deal. That didn't go well with breakfast so I watched cartoons. At 9:30 I was showered, shaved, and out the door on the way to Barnes and Noble. No tail today.

It was a nice day, my lament at there no longer being a mom and pop bookstore here anymore had vanished (but not completely), and I enjoyed it very much. I accepted the fact I was in some ways trendy and had coffee and started reading one of the astronomy magazines I had bought. I noticed a beautiful young woman and when our eyes met, she smiled. I ended up having coffee with her. She had purchased a book on Leopold and Loeb of which I had read a lot about and we got into a conversation.

I sensed the interest and as always my heart jumped at the thought of an attractive woman wanting to spend time with me. This was surprising. It had been a while. I almost said to her that I was dealing with a big loss but didn't. I also thought about telling her I had killed someone with my bare hands, and for god's sake I have no idea why that popped into my head. Cory James. She was 28 and worked for the City Department of Finance and was going to school at night to finish her degree in Criminal Justice and would be taking the LSATs—the test necessary to go to Law School—in the Fall. I did point out I was a good deal older and she shushed me so I laughed. We had coffee and talked about Leopold and Loeb and Darrow representing them.

"It's there that I believe the myth about prison justice started."

"What do you mean?"

"Most of the public, even some of the people that

work in prisons, have this idea that there is an army of righteous wrongfully convicted cons that dole out justice to baby rapers and people like that."

"Oh. I kinda thought there was."

"No. It works out sometimes that way but not for the reasons you'd think. When it comes down to it not every baby raper looks like Woody Allen. Some of them are hard. Strong. There was one guy in New York used to literally split kids up the middle. He was also five foot six and about two hundred and fifty pounds of rock solid muscle. And he knew how to use a knife really well. Even the cops said when they arrested him, 'Wait till they get him in the shower.' After he killed the first three inmates, no one went near him."

"And Leopold and Loeb?"

"Loeb was big and strong. He owed some guy money. He disrespected him and told him to go fuck himself. The guy killed him. At first he said it was because of what Loeb did to Bobby Franks, later he admitted he did it because Loeb owed him money and insulted him. You let someone walk over you in prison and everyone walks over you in prison."

"And Leopold?"

"Comparatively small and weak. But a lot of money. He lived as well as you could in prison. He could pay for protection."

She had light brown skin and dark brown, almost black eyes. She didn't have any kids, she worked full time, went to school part time and apparently, unless my eyes were failing, spent a good deal of time in the gym. She worked on her childhood friend's political campaign as well, and her dad was apparently having a tough time after a fall. She was on winter break from school and we agreed to have dinner the day after tomorrow. She gave me her address as well as her number and told me to call when I got there and she'd come down. I watched her leave but of course my thoughts went to Mandy.

I went to Sal's house for the 3pm dinner, arriving early and having a few beers. His wife kissed me hello, and I complimented her on how she looked. The house smelled wonderful. She had grape leaves and deviled eggs out and I felt my normal appetite kick in. His two kids ignored me, which only the best people do, and I gave them their presents and got a couple of kisses and then they went back to ignoring me. Sal gave me a cold Stella Artois and we went into his backyard. It was about 45 degrees, not too cold.

We talked a little while he smoked a cigarette.

He asked me how things were. "The word unbalanced comes to mind," I said. "But I am functioning."

He nodded. His neighbors had two dogs and both of them were out. One of them was disabled. The other, a very good natured yellow lab, was trotting around and stopped to look at Sal and I and wagged his tail furiously.

"Need anything?" he asked.

"No, man, I'm good."

He had invited me to bring Molly. I was worried that as people were going in and out there might be an opportunity for her to get out. I regretted not bringing her.

He was concerned about me. He needed to know I was okay but he would stop there. We had been friends for almost as long as we were alive. Despite having a job and a family, and going to school, he had been around a lot the last few months. So had my brothers and a few other people. At first I wasn't overly receptive, but they stuck it out to make sure I was okay. Chief Mariano had stopped by a few times, twice on duty and three times off duty. He and his wife had me over for dinner a few times. I got a delivery: four baskets of Italian food and pastries from Eddie Siciliano. I also got a gift wrapped bottle of McCallan Rare Cask Single Malt that just said Tempesta on it. Both Siciliano and Tempesta came to the wake. Jimmy Hannan, Joe Lavelle, Tito Alvarez, and Bobby Bianchi all came together. That night we closed Duffy's. There were people on line to get into the wake. Shane tried hard to be strong.

At some point I got hold of John Harrington, another attorney from the building, and he set up some kind of account for me where I could make regular contributions to it and it could be used for college or starting a business. I got Shane a telescope for his birthday.

It was hard to say for sure but it looked like the bullet changed trajectory when it hit Mandy and went up a little, enough that it missed several possible vital areas in my chest and ended up going through my shoulder.

I got home early, let Molly out, and fed her and the cat. I knew that the cat was alive as the food from the morning had disappeared and the litter box needed cleaning. I consoled myself that this was because he was originally a feral and went out of his way to avoid me. Can't fault him for that. I gave Molly some of the food from the huge plate Michelle had given me when I left Sal's. I was still stuffed.

Although I liked the feel of a book and had also

gotten into audio books for while in the car, I had a
kindle and there was a PI series. I was partly who I was
because of reading PI novels as a kid. Mike Hammer,
Spenser, Sam Spade, Phillip Marlowe, Archie Goodwin,
and Nero Wolfe. Rounded out by a few that were sadly
lesser known to modern readers like Race Williams.
Andrew Vachss' Burke, who I got to in my early twenties
after I started working as a PI myself, had the honorary
title. It was dark and often a hard read because it was
real. My real life role models were cut from the same
cloth as my literary heroes.

I had planned on reading that evening and settled
on the PI novel. By chapter three I had thrown up in my
mouth a little. By chapter five I had done something I
never did before and returned it to Kindle. I knew how
hard writing was. I'd tried it once or twice. I never gave a
book a bad review. This was a series that was being
carried on after the original writer had died. The character had been apolitical. Now the character was woke. I
had forgiven inaccuracies and mistakes here and there
in the prior novels, like a pro who was checking his gun
to see if it was loaded prior to a bad situation and the
main character calling a semi-automatic rifle an assault
weapon. The hero of the story was the cleaned up,
fantasy version of an air head politician whose brain
couldn't jump start a Duracell. If you wanted to put your
politics into your character, fine. If it bothered me I
wouldn't read it, but changing a literary icon—that was
in poor taste.

"You could have done a better job," I said to Molly.
By the thumping of her tail, she agreed. I put the TV on.
Svengoolie was a repeat of "The Monolith Monsters." A
favourite of mine. I watched MeTV till I fell asleep

sometime during "Lost in Space." An example of sad passage into adulthood was realizing if I had been John Robinson, I'd have shoved Dr. Smith out the airlock by episode four.

I went to bed, shoulder threatening to wake me completely, but I slept until four. I woke up crying. I didn't remember exactly why but there was only one thing that would have caused that. Molly woke up and came from the end of the bad and nestled into me. I fell asleep again after a while.

3

I was up early and took my cardio in the form of a walk with Molly at Clove Lakes. My embarrassment at her wearing a bright doggie sweater Cheryl got her was eclipsed by the temperature. Although it was warm for January, it was still January, early winter. It was almost fifty degrees but when we were out of the sunlight and with the breeze it was cold. I got back to the house, stretched and showered.

I was lonely. I talked to Mandy all the time. She never answered. Maybe I wasn't listening the right way. I thought about hitting the bag a while but my shoulder vociferously protested the idea. I took a pill and an anti-inflammatory that would turn my stomach into an acid vat that Vincent Price would have dropped someone into. I didn't feel like making breakfast. I had rye toast and some yogurt to lessen the effect of the aforementioned anti-inflammatory.

Tomorrow I was in the office in the morning and I was scheduled at 2PM to testify on the divorce case that generated the tail. That would be fun. I'd brought my notes home but I really didn't need to review them. I recalled vividly the nonsense on that case. I had a long career, and Diane Cretella was a standout to say the least. I shook my head. That poor kid was being tortured because the judge was partial to the mother having custody, based on her sex. Truth was—no studies here, just my recollection and experience—most of the time that was true. If they couldn't work together for the sake of the kids, most of the time the mother ended up being best to raise the kids. Not always, and it's a problem when cases are not decided on their individual merits. When that happens sometimes, oftentimes, the kids ended up paying the price.

In this case, Diane had put her two-year-old daughter on a fad diet because she looked fat. The child, according to three different physicians, was normal weight and healthy.

I was trying to figure out what to do with myself when the phone rang. It was Cory, the girl from Barnes & Noble.

"Hi," she said. Her voice sounded like Spring and it immediately cheered me up.

"Hi back," I said. Clever, was I.

"I know we said tomorrow night but I wondered if by any chance you might be free this morning? I ended up being free but, I kind of want to talk with you about something, a problem a friend is having, if you don't mind giving me some advice." I smiled, her voice was confident but there was an edge to it, like she was worried I might say no. I knew that edge because I'd felt it myself from time to time. I have been very fortunate in the women I have known, but I never knew what they saw in me.

"Well, Miss, I happen to be free. What did you have in mind?"

"Late breakfast or brunch?"

"Love to. Do you have a preference?"

"I wouldn't want to infringe on your masculinity, sir." She giggled as she said that.

I laughed. "Wow, to be that wise for such a tender age. The restaurant at The Hilton Hotel serves a great brunch. Half past noon give you enough time?"

"Perfect. I love it there!"

"Great, see you there."

"Okay. See you there. Bye."

"Bye."

Damn. It looked at this point like it was going to be a good day. Turns out that wasn't an entirely good guess. Just a few hours later, I would be in handcuffs.

Truck was on his own today but, there he sat, two houses down from me. I picked out the PT Cruiser from my window. I lost him in about ten seconds.

Richard and Lois Nicotra were shaking hands with people at the entrance to the restaurant. They owned all of the huge office complexes on either side of South Ave. I knew them casually, Richard a little more so. He smiled and we greeted each other by name. I had made a reservation, and now it was twelve-thirty on the dot. As I walked through the door I turned as someone put a hand on my arm. It was Cory. Damn again. She had looked great in Barnes and Noble but now she was stunning. She was wearing a light black coat, a pink blouse, and painted on jeans. I smiled and bent down and she kissed me on the cheek. That just happened and it happened right.

"Hi there, handsome!" she beamed. "You look great."

"Says the beautiful woman on whom every pair of eyes in this place now rests." She smiled and looked down a little.

I knew the maître d. He seated us right away by the window. Brunch was buffet or special order. A waiter came over and told us the specials and the options.

"Mimosa? Bloody Mary?" I asked her.

"I'd love a Mimosa."

"Okay, give us a few minutes on the food. One Mimosa, one Bloody Mary Spicy, two coffees."

"Cream or sugar?"

I raised my eyebrows and looked at her.

"Cream," she said, smiling. I nodded to the waiter.

I took off my brown suede sports jacket and put it on the back of the chair. I was wearing a black turtle neck and black jeans. I was of course on call this week and I had my Glock 45 under the turtle neck. I sat facing the door and the slight bulge faced the window. The restaurant was crowded but the tables were far enough apart. We both opted for the buffet and got up together for it. At my suggestion we talked about her friend's problem first. In short, her friend, the politician she mentioned, was running for re-election. It appeared she was being blackmailed or rather her fiancé was.

"I asked her a few times if there was something wrong and she kept telling me no. Apparently they are threatening to go to the media. She was upset yesterday and she didn't want to tell me on the phone."

"I can meet with her tomorrow, if you like."

"Would you? Do you think you can help her?"

"Probably, but I'd have to know more about it."

"Is it confidential, if she talks to you?"

"If you mean privileged, like with an attorney or a

doctor, then no, not in this state. However, if she is worried about that, then her attorney can hire me."

"So the attorney's privilege with her extends to you if you work for the attorney?"

"Exactly. Very good," I complimented her.

She politely asked if she could text her friend. I smiled and said yes. She sent the message and then we had our first real conversation.

The conversation was good. She didn't have any kids, her mom had passed and her dad wasn't doing well. She lived with him. The food was good. We had finished the food; of course I had gotten my money's worth and refilled the plate twice. She only refilled hers partially once.

A younger man, well-muscled and dressed trendy, walked in the room. He was scanning the crowd. He looked angry. His gaze settled on the back of Cory's head and he walked over. He looked Hispanic to me, light skinned. His jaw was clenched. I scanned him as he walked over. He was maybe two inches taller than me. I had at least forty pounds on him. Near as I could tell he wasn't carrying anything but no real way to be sure.

"It appears you have a visitor," I said to her. I indicated with a nod toward him. She looked. Her expression was shock at first but she recovered quickly. She was angry and embarrassed.

"Who is this," he said to her, staring at me.

"Leave here," she said to him. "We have been broken up for months. It doesn't matter who this man is, and it's none of your business."

"Is that right?" he asked. People were beginning to look.

"Is that right, pops?" he asked me. I smiled. "Is it none of my business?"

"It does look that way, sonny," I said.

"I'm not your son, motherfucker," he snarled at me.

"Clearly not because you wouldn't be speaking that way. I'd have washed your mouth out with soap."

He was a prick and he was a bully, and he was nervous. However, he had apparently decided to make a stand.

"Please just go," Cory said to him.

"Will you call me later?"

"No."

"You fucking cunt. I give you everything and you turn your back on me. You gonna go fuck this senior citizen now?"

"Time to go, kid," I told him. I stood up. Cory got upset.

"It's okay," she said. "I don't want this. I'm sorry, I should—"

"Hey," I said to her, ignoring Romeo. "You have nothing to be sorry for. Do you want to go with this guy?" I asked.

"No, but—" she started.

"Time for you to go, kid," I said.

"Fuck you, Grandpa," he said. He grabbed her arm, hard. She gasped and tried to pull away. I closed the gap and caught him with the heel of my right palm and he let go of her, stumbling back. He recovered in a quicker time than I'd have thought and moved toward me. I shuffled in and caught him on the side of his face with a very hard left hook. I didn't pull back much. I let him have most of it. I won't lie, it felt fucking great. He dropped like a stone, and the tooth behind his right incisor and a wash of blood came out of his mouth. He was breathing okay but he was out.

Everyone in the restaurant froze. The maître d had started over when he grabbed Cory. He was a few feet short when I hit Romeo. He stopped and looked at me.

"Call for the cops and an ambulance," I told him.

"Done, Jimmy," he said.

I patted Romeo down as best I could and didn't find anything. He had landed face down and I didn't want to move him. I shook my head and sighed. I sat, took my gun out under the table, ejected the round from the chamber. I put that on the table under the napkin, and I took the magazine out and slid both under the napkin. Cory didn't see the bullet but she saw that. Her eyes got a little wider. Surprise not revulsion, I hoped. I unlocked my phone, adjusted it so it wouldn't lock again. I took my wallet out, put my driver's license, state ID, and carry permit on the table as well.

"Listen," I said to her softly. "I am sorry that happened I front of you. I couldn't let him put his hands on you and try to take you out of here. The cops are going to come. If it doesn't go well with them for some reason I will tell you to make the call. Then I want you to open my phone's address book to Chief Mariano, call him, and tell him what happened, okay?"

"Yeah," she said. Her eyes teared up a little. "I'm so sorry." She cast her eyes down. I reached over the table and touched her face and gently lifted her chin.

"You did absolutely nothing to be sorry for, sweetheart. I promise it will all be okay."

Romeo groaned.

"As far as he goes," I said, nodding toward the still immobile Romeo, "I don't know the story but from this point forward unless you want him in it, he is out of your life and I will see to it."

"I don't want anything to do with him but I can't ask you to..." Her eyes were down again.

"Hey," I said softly. She looked up. "You didn't ask. I offered. No strings." I head sirens. "My fiancée had someone like him in her life."

She looked shocked. "Your..."

"I'm sorry, sweetheart, we haven't really had a chance to talk. She was killed."

The cops came in. A tall lanky guy and a tall woman, about my height. They immediately assessed the situation. The ambulance people were attending Romeo. I told the cops what was under the napkin. The tall cop told me to put my hands on my head and turn around.

Cory jumped up. "Wait! He didn't—"

I stopped her again, and as I complied with the directions, told her, "It's okay."

"Should I—" she started.

"No. Not yet."

Once they had me cuffed, they asked me what happened and I told them. The female cop started talking to the other patrons, some of whom were very shook up.

"You're Creed, right?" the tall cop asked me. "You killed Stanton last year?"

"Yeah."

"You appear to be a magnet for trouble," he said.

"Well I can't sing or dance..."

When Cory heard the cop mention Stanton, I saw another look of surprise on her face. Damn. Not a good "Damn" this time. I wanted to tell her about that.

"Listen, for a minute if you would," I said to the cop as the female cop made her way back. "He came in, angry. He grabbed her and tried to take her out of here. I knocked him off her and he stepped toward me. I know everyone says it is self-defense, but it was. People here should back that up. If you want a reference, Mike Mariano is a friend.

"You know Chief Mariano?" the female cop asked. Her last name was apparently Harden, as per the ID tag.

"His home, cell, and work number are in my phone."

"The people I spoke to so far, including the host, back him up," Harden told her partner, whose name, also discovered in similar fashion, was Glass.

"If you take the cuffs off I give you my word, I will just sit. My date is upset as it is."

"Care to elaborate more on your story?"

"It's exactly what I said," I told him. "Nothing more to say."

"No history with him?" Meaning did we know of each other before hand and was there animosity.

"None, and I know you'd find out if there was, so no point in me lying," I said.

They looked at me and then each other. Glass nodded and Harden uncuffed me. I sat as I said I would. Glass took the gun and accessories. A woman came over and took out her cell phone and spoke to the cops. Romeo was regaining coherence.

An older woman had taken video from cell phone and came up to show the cops. She showed them her phone and the video of the incident. Another cop car came and a sergeant showed up. I knew him. Dennis

Frank. I smiled broadly as he came in and he burst out laughing.

"What the fuck did you do now, Jimmy?" he said as he came up and shook my hand. His driver, the two cops, and Cory all looked at us.

"Me, do? Sergeant Frank I acted with the utmost of civility and," I paused, "I don't know, insert some word in there." We both laughed.

"He tried to take my friend out of here by force, and when I removed him from her he came at me," I said.

"Witnesses and video seem to back him up, Sarge," Harden said.

When I told Dennis about what happened, and what he did he told the responding officers I was free to go, and he rattled off a bunch of charges for Romeo. He looked over to Romeo and stared for a minute. The ambulance attendants had put him on the gurney and were about to wheel him out. He was in and out of sleep. Probably a concussion.

"Wait," Dennis told the ambulance attendants. His countenance, posture, and character went hard. He said it softly but they stopped. He walked over and looked down at Romeo. He reached and grabbed his belt buckle. He started wiggling it, Romeo groaned and tried to push his hand away and Dennis slapped it. After wiggling a few more seconds, he pulled the belt buckle knife out. It looked razor sharp.

"Cuff him to the gurney," he told his driver. "Add that to the list of charges," Dennis said.

A concealed knife of that type might as well be a gun for all intents and purposes in New York, as far as potential weight in charges. He told the cops to go to the hospital after they got the names, addresses, and phone numbers of the witnesses.

I caught the name of the woman who had the cell phone video. The way things were, who knew if I would get a lawsuit out of this. I noticed she had the same kind of phone I had. I went up to her and apologized for what happened.

She told me, "I wish my daughter dated men like you. He got what he deserved, son of a bitch. Is your girlfriend okay?"

"Yes," I said and thanked her again.

I asked her if I could have her phone and copy the video to mine. I mentioned in case of a lawsuit and she agreed, handing me her phone. I thanked her, did so, and gave her back her phone. She sat back down with an older man who was apparently her husband.

"Good hook, young man," he said.

I grinned, thanked him, and walked back. Young man and old man in the same day. *It's all a matter of perspective*, I thought.

The cops were all gathered again. I went over there, and we talked a little. Cory drifted over. She seemed unsure. I moved my head, indicating when she should come over. She took my hand, hesitantly at first. I held it firmly. She had seen a lot and wasn't expecting it.

"We are all good, Jimmy," Dennis said. "You can go."

Cory asked, "Why did you have to cuff him?"

"May I?" I asked the cops. Dennis nodded.

"Honey, all they knew for sure when they got here was I had hurt your ex. He was unconscious, and I was a potential threat to them. They did right. They controlled the situation, and when they found out what happened, they acted accordingly." The cops nodded in agreement.

"Ohhhhh," she said.

"Everyone says its self-defense," Harden said. "It rarely is."

"He apparently put that guy down with one really good punch, according to the witnesses. I want to go home without having my brains scrambled," Glass said. "Even if he didn't know the Chief and the Sarge, everyone backed him up."

"What if he didn't have a lot of witnesses?" she asked.

"He articulates himself well, and what the people he knows know about him, he'd probably be okay. Depends on the cops that showed up. Often the guy that is standing is the one that goes."

"Oh God," she said.

"It's how things are," I said.

"But if you know Mariano?" she asked.

"Everyone knows the Chief," Harden said. "If he said we could take this guy at his word it would be truth. He wouldn't tell us not to lock him up, but if he vouches for someone, then he is telling the truth."

"Not a lot of people like that left," Glass said.

I thanked the cops and they were gracious. Glass and Harden had warmed up a little and I made a mental note to write a letter praising their actions to their precinct commander. I was about to leave and I stopped, and Dennis knew right away why.

"Can I tell them?" I asked him, grinning.

"You would have anyway, Jimmy Boy," he said grinning back.

"I once broke your sergeant's nose." They all looked blank for a second and then everyone laughed.

"He also kicked my leg so hard I couldn't walk without limping for two weeks."

I re-armed myself and we walked out. I apologized to Arnie, the maître d, and the Nicotras, for what happened and they all waved it off. We walked into the parking lot.

"Where's your car?"

"I Ubered," she said.

"Listen, I can take you home, we can sit and talk in my car if you want, or we can go back to my place and talk. Whatever you feel comfortable with."

She looked at me. I think if it had been normal circumstances there would be a smile on her face but she still looked a little edgy.

"We can go to your place."

I walked with her to my car, opened the door, and she got in.

I got in and drove us back to the house. Five minutes later we were inside and six minutes later she was in love with Molly. The cat actually made a brief appearance. It had clouded up outside and got a little colder. I asked if she wanted something to drink and she said yes. I asked what and she said surprise me.

I made her coffee, which at the restaurant I learned she took with cream and no sugar, and I made myself some. I poured two glasses of Goldschläger and put it all on a tray and brought it in. She was petting Molly and talking to her.

"I really am sorry," she began as I sat down. "I had no idea. He knew I liked that place and he must have gone looking for me. My Dad must have taken the car, and he figured I wasn't home."

"First off, again sweetheart, and I mean this, you did nothing wrong. You have nothing to apologize for. I am sorry you had to see something that violent. That's not the kind of thing you want as atmosphere for a first date."

She smiled. "I watched him push someone around once, a homeless guy. It's why I left him. Just a feeling he wasn't showing me who he really was."

"He is a bully and probably a predator."

"So Mandy," she said her name gently. "She had kind of the same problem I have."

"It's not uncommon, sweetheart. Thank God you care enough about yourself and broke it off."

"My dad will want to kill him," she said.

"Well you will get an OP out of it and that may help. Do you think he will keep after you?" I asked.

"I don't think so. The one guy he pushed around was an older weak man. He seemed aggressive to women, like waitresses and stuff. He was generally nice to me but he slipped up a few times. What he called his sense of humor was always belittling and cruel. I broke it off with him after Thanksgiving. I had dinner at his house and he was outright mean to his mom."

She told me about their relationship and ending it. And how her dad was sick, but he had been a very strong man. She was bright and sweet. Lovely inside and out. I liked her very much but I also felt guilty. Mandy would want me to be happy. I knew that. Easier said than done. I told her about everything that happened. Mandy, killing Stanton, the freaks. Molly got off the couch and went to her water dish. She paused and looked at the water, which I knew was fresh, and then curled up on her bed and went to sleep. I recalled Spenser in a novel once saying, "The ways of dogs are often mysterious, or are often a mystery." I was trying to remember the exact quote when Cory snuggled in next to me and rested her head on my chest.

She kissed me and I kissed her back and it became more passionate and there was need from both of us. I carried her upstairs, and we got to know each other, much more in depth than I would have thought, this morning.

We lay there after and she spoke softly.

"I don't want you to think the wrong thing. I like you a lot. I wanted you when I saw you and I'm lonely. I love what you did for me but I wasn't with you because of that."

"I know that," I said. "I wouldn't want anyone to be with me out of obligation. And I'm with you on this regardless of where things go with us. I wanted you, too. I need to go slow. You are the first woman I've been with since..." I had trouble there for a second. "She died." I finished. "It's still very hard for me," I said.

"Going slow is fine," she said. "We aren't talking about going slow with what we just—"

Before she could finish that I had her in my arms again, and she laughed. I liked her laugh. If her voice on the phone was Spring, her laugh was Summer. A cool summer evening after a hot day, by the water as the sun began to set.

She stayed with me until evening. She had to go and make food for her dad. I took her home and enjoyed her company every minute of the ride. Damn.

4

THE NEXT DAY was normal in that almost nothing that was planned happened. Jeff was in before me. I said hi to the girls and grabbed coffee and went into his office. No tail.

"How are things?" I asked.

"Going well. Rita called and said court is postponed today. She will have a court date later."

"Okay. Well, I was hoping to get the damned thing over with today. I have to call Rita. I picked up a tail on New Years' Eve," I said.

His eyebrows went up. "Oh?"

"Yeah." I gave him the rundown.

"Desperation," he said.

"Yeah." I nodded. "We also have an out of office consult tonight with a local politician. I'm waiting for the details. I got it covered, if you like. No need for both of us to be there."

"I'd appreciate that. The wife has a doctor's appointment tonight."

"No problem at all."

We drank coffee and went over things including active cases and a few meetings later for the week.

I had a long talk with Rita about the tail and I asked if she could give me a little time to come up with something, and I mentioned a few possibilities. She liked it and told me the next court date was a month away. The rest of the day was S.O.B. until I met Cory's friends.

I had arranged with Cory by text for her to meet me at the office at five. We'd grab a quick bite at the coffee shop and she'd fill me in on what she learned and about Evy, as her friends called her.

I had a turkey burger with a hard fried egg on top and she had a salad. In the interest of still having a view of my toes, I had a salad instead of the fries. Which could have come with gravy. Or melted cheese. Or have been criss cut. Or I could have had Balsamic vinegar with it. Or I could have had ketchup. Any one of those ways would have made me much happier. I looked at Cory and forgot about it for a second.

"What are you smiling about, sir?" she asked me, returning the smile.

"I have a superb memory."

"And what are you remembering?"

"You naked and crying out in ecstasy."

She laughed and blushed.

"I could postpone the consult," I said to her.

"We should have enough time for both," she said.

"Not if I keep on schedule."

She looked at me quizzically.

"I have to increase the number of climaxes you experience each time or I feel I haven't done what I should."

She giggled. "I approve of your principles."

"You are delightful, dear girl," I said to her. "My sky has been nothing but gray for a long time now and you made it lighter."

She reached across the table and took my hand. "You did the same."

We had coffee after and she told me about Evy. Of course if you followed the media, you'd know who she was. She had been elected to Congress on Staten Island, the only conservative of the five boroughs. But often, people went with who they thought were the better candidates. Politically it was like anywhere else. A lot of promises, few fulfilled. She and her campaign manager, both single, were an item. He was some kind of online entrepreneur. That stood out from memory; there was lot of speculation he was the driving force behind the campaign.

The party people had control for the most part and hated outsiders, the idea of the party (either of them) serving their constituents and not the other way around had no play with them. Evy had served in the military and had gotten in on a strong grassroots campaign. She was an outsider to both parties but as usual it appeared she had often said whatever she felt would get her in, regardless of her actual views.

Her actual views could be summed up by the Che T shirt she wore often. She had already broken a number of promises, been against a Walmart opening on the Island, and a lot of jobs were lost because of that. How much influence she actually had over that was debatable but there were a lot of grumblings from people who needed work. I was anticipating threats of some kind.

"You never told me anything about your political

beliefs," she said as the waitress brought cheesecake for me and two forks.

"I tend towards fiscal conservatism."

She smiled. "Could you elaborate a little on that?"

"I don't care who sleeps with who, I believe in the ability to speak freely which does not release you from the consequences of said action. I don't care what you identify as. If what you do doesn't affect me or hurt other people, it's your business."

"So even Nazis, child molesters, etc. can say what they want."

"Absolutely. NAMBLA is the North American Man Boy Love Association. They believe raping a child is an act of love. I'm happy they get a chance to speak their minds because 99 percent of the population will reject it out of hand. I'd prefer the freaks in the open. I don't want them underground. I want the cops to know exactly who to go to when a kid goes missing. The Supreme Court weighed in on free speech. If you incite violence you are liable for consequences. Ever read *Mein Kampf*?" I asked.

"No."

"Preposterous, ludicrous, and outright racist."

"So why read it?"

"So you know what you are actually up against. So you know what motivated people to stand by and watch 6 million people slaughtered and another 50 million dead world-wide at the end of World War Two. The problem is people don't learn or they are cowards or both. The last thing you want to do is shut those people down. And to be honest, I prefer my Nazis to wear the swastika. It helps to identify them. Claiming you are something other than a nazi and acting like one, that doesn't fly."

"I never looked at it that way. Shouldn't there be rules?"

"Of course. Children shouldn't read that garbage. They shouldn't be sexualized, or fed indoctrination of any kind. They are children for such a short period of time and it never comes back. But as they grow older, you can't shield them too much. The world can be a hard place. You don't get a fighter ready for a boxing match if he doesn't spar."

She nodded. "And the fiscal part?"

"Money can be much better spent. The last borough president allotted seventy-five thousand dollars for a patch of land to be kept up that the state and federal government disputed who was responsible for. It turns out the upkeep was mowing the grass every two weeks in an area smaller than a football field. I can think of a lot of places that 75k could have been better put to use. It went to a campaign supporter of his."

"How much food could that have bought?"

"Exactly."

"Does it bother you that Evy is a Socialist?"

"Nope." I smiled. "It might have bothered me twenty years ago if she lied about being a socialist to get in, which she did, but now I expect a politician to lie upon opening their mouth. And that includes both parties."

"But you don't agree with it."

"Socialism?"

"Yeah."

"It is doomed to fail. It never worked, it will never work. The only excuse is it was never real socialism. Try that with heart surgery. It works great on paper but the reason it has never worked is human nature. And the reason it keeps failing is that the people that keep trying to implement it are not better than the people that tried before."

"Why is it still around?"

"People are lied to about it and in many cases it sounds good and there is a genuine desire to help. For others it's a path to power. The other problem is no one that tries to implement it is in reality any better or smarter than the people that tried before. Even if by some miracle they were flawless, the people around them—the Stalins, the Pol Pots, the Maos, the Castros— will just kill them and take over."

"Then why would you help her?"

"Well, presuming I can and she deserves it, one, it's my profession. Two, she is entitled to think what she wants. Better people than I have fallen for it. Hemingway for example."

She nodded thoughtfully.

"And three," I smiled. "Because you asked me to." She slid her hand across the table again and held mine for a few seconds. I really was getting attached to her. She asked questions to know the answers. That is rarer than it ought to be.

"Why, if it's a profession, does deserve it come into play."

"Good question. It's more that I have rules. If helping her doesn't violate them, then I do."

"Who wouldn't you work for?"

"Not a lot of people. I have worked for people who have committed murder."

"How does that—"

"I also believe in due process. Guilt by accusation is

a dangerous road to travel. I have worked for people that have been accused of molesting children."

"My God, how hard is that?"

"Very. But until a conviction it's just an accusation, and it would be worth noting, two of the three cases I worked in in the last 5 years, the people were innocent. But the attorneys I work for know I won't pull strings or try to help someone out of a jam if they actually hurt the kids. And there are degrees."

"Give me an example."

"It's a different penalty for flashing someone at a bus stop than it is for rape. If a kid commits a crime, punishment should be part of the answer often, but there should also be a genuine attempt to help the kid. If you throw a kid into prison and he or she survives, if there's no intervention, what comes out will be worse. There was a girl, sold off when she was a little kid. She was a prostituted child," I started. "When you say "child prostitute" it implies consent. No child is capable of giving consent," I said, answering her question. She nodded.

"So at 16 I believe she loses it and shoots a john in the head. These so called "father's rights" people or "Men's rights" people go nuts screaming for a life sentence. There's multiple problems with that. One, a normal 16-year-old is a pinhead, they don't know anything. Their moral compass is still developing. Do we expect a kid, sold as a sex slave, to have a properly developed moral compass at 16? And to be honest I don't care much about a perp that paid to rape a child. Should punishment be involved? Maybe. But putting her away for life? With no attempt to help her? That's the system failing her twice."

"Like the Central Park Rape kids?"

"No. Similar circumstances in that they were children. But the victim was an innocent woman, jogging. They took the cops to the scene and described in detail what they did to her. Those guys were not exonerated. The charges were vacated. There's a difference. In my mind anyway. Punishment should have been part of the crime but also, they were kids that did something horrific. They should have been punished but an attempt should have been made to help them. Out committing rape at 16...I'm betting there isn't much of a home life there. It's the reason kids join gangs. The gangs are family, they belong."

She nodded, considering. "Cory, what is important is that each case is looked at individually. We can't even approach having an actual justice system until that happens."

"Does race play into it?"

"It depends. Historically, more black kids are poor, and poor people have a disadvantage in the system. So do middle class people but that's another issue. I don't see, nor should anyone see color when the perp is that young. They should see kids. They damned well should see kids when they are victims. Does that bother you?" I asked her.

"No, it kind of makes sense. Some people think because I'm black, part of me anyway, that I'm supposed to believe certain things. I find that offensive."

"You should. May I ask out curiosity what the rest of your genetic makeup is? To produce such beauty, it must be exceptional."

She smiled brilliantly. "My dad is Cuban and African. My mom was mostly Indian with some

Chinese in her. Her family moved here from Mumbai and she met my dad by chance."

"Well you are striking, dear lady. Beauty is an understatement and does not do you justice."

"I'm curious. Am I the first, um, nonwhite girl you've been with?"

"Nope."

She smiled devilishly. "And how many women have you been with?"

"Nope." I answered again and we both laughed.

"Well, clearly you learned what you needed to," she said and giggled a little.

"Well, given I heard you cry out that you thought you were going to die twice," I said and she laughed again.

"Okay, were you taught these things?" she asked, shifting the conversation back. "I mean your views. Were they like your dad's or someone else's?"

"No. It comes from observation."

"God, I bet you hate your work sometimes."

"Sometimes it's hard. But in general I love what I do." *Except when it costs the woman you love her life*, that voice said.

We talked a little more and I paid the check and headed out to meet Evy and her fiancé. In the car she told me what she knew about the help Evy needed. I checked and there was the PT Cruiser on the corner and the Dodge Charger. It hit me. This numbskull was following me. Rita didn't know why they needed the delay; the attorney representing Diane Cretella had supposedly been ill. They got the damned delay so they could follow me. They were across the street near the

office and had to cross Manor Road which was busy. I'd
ended up parking.

I made a right hand turn and sped up a bit and
made another right, and then one more and took that
down the end of the block and pulled in on the side of
the road. I waited five minutes.

Cory looked at me questioningly. "I have someone
tailing me. Hired by someone on the opposite side of a
case. They are losing the case and hoping they get
something bad on me as I am a key witness. It's nothing
to worry about. I'm trying to figure on how to use this to
my advantage. Tell me more about why Evy needs
help."

"She looked very upset one day an email had come
to her private account. She said someone was trying to
blackmail her fiancé."

"Let me guess, the significant other has money?"

"How did you know that?" she asked.

"Easy. Half the socialist advocates do." I snickered.
"And it was online. He ran her campaign and helped get
her elected."

"And the other half?" she asked with a smile. "Of the
socialists, I mean."

"They figure on being in the Politburo," I said. "Any
idea what he was being blackmailed for?"

"No, but Evy was worried."

"How about Evy?" I asked. "Does she have money?"

"Not really. She wasn't as poor as she made out, but
she went to college on scholarships, her parents helped
her, and she worked. She always had a good home. She
grew up in the Westerleigh area."

Westerleigh was a better neighborhood than I grew
up in or was in now. Middle class, low crime, and some

beautiful parks. I sighed and shook my head. If you believed her campaign ads she was "from the streets."

"What is her degree in?"

"Political Science." Cory smiled as I laughed like hell and we drove away.

EVY AND RICHARD were waiting in the Congresswoman's (Congressperson?) office. I asked her to go in ahead of me and called Rita and told the tail was still ongoing and why I thought that was.

"Jesus that is grasping at straws," she said.

"Well, Ms. Viola, you pretty much backed them into a corner so the judge is somewhat hostile toward us."

"That is an understatement," she said.

"I believe I actually heard you say on the record that if Diane was the husband based on her conduct, she'd be relegated to supervised visits the rest of her life. That could not have endeared you to the judge."

"Well, it was called for. If we end up with anything less than full custody and decision making rights, I'm appealing. They know this. And I'll win. The Law Guardian is on our side, or rather, more correctly, the child's side. I should tell you this, this horror show on the other side called you a murderer in chambers and likely, rather than face her own client's short comings and issues or take the blame herself, blamed you."

I was quiet. And I was angry. I had seen how the mother was treating the child first hand while escorting my client to pick the child up. Her neglect and maltreatment of that child were well documented. I didn't mind the term murderer. It was self-defense, but there was no question at all that I'd have killed him regardless after he took Mandy from me. I objected to the term, feeling like it cheapened her memory. Apparently these thoughts rolled around in my head a while because I got a text from Cory asking if I'd be much longer.

I walked into the office and Cory met me. It was late and everyone had gone home except for Evy and Garrett Thomas. I was a little taken aback when I saw how fair her complexion was. In her pictures, she looked much darker skinned. She did have that bearing most retired military people had. Her campaign manager, alleged paramour and Chief of Staff, Garrett Thomas was about my height and he looked trim like he worked out to be fit. There was a picture of him in a martial arts uniform on the wall, competing in what looked like a tournament.

They offered me coffee or soda. Garret hinted at something stronger. I had read single malts were trendy now, and I bet myself five bucks that was what he hinted at. I appreciatively declined but accepted water. Cory went to get it and we all ended up sitting at a conference room table. Cory sat next to me and Evy and Garrett sat on the opposite side.

"I'm in a hotly contested race," she said. "I present a danger to the establishment, because I stand against climate change and I stand for the rich paying their share."

I smiled.

"It's not right that people should try to silence me because I stand for certain things," she said.

"I agree completely on that point," I said.

She smiled; Garret said nothing.

"I do need to know what is wrong, so that I will know if I can and how to help you," I said to them.

"Do you guys want me to step out?" Cory asked.

"No, that's okay. We trust you, but no one else knows," Garret said.

"If necessary I can work through your attorney and that would maintain privilege. If not I can sign something that says unless compelled to divulge by a judge or law enforcement, providing they can demonstrate to me what I'm working on is relevant to what they are, but in that instance they can compel me."

"I have an attorney on stand by and a fax machine he can send you a letter to. I can put you on the phone with him. He has been my attorney for years."

I told him that would be fine and gave him my cell number which he texted to someone. I spoke with a corporate lawyer, Brendan (last name something he said too fast for a human to understand, belonging to a firm that had six thousand four hundred and eleven names in it) who talked a mile a minute and referred to Garret as "The Big G." I automatically turned the wince into a smile. The stereotypical progressive hipster was as dismaying to me as the Jersey Shore persona that everyone outside of Staten Island seemed to think the Island was populated with. He called "The Big G" and said G left the conference room and walked out talking. From my phone I emailed him my normal retainer. He called me back, made a few acceptable changes, and sent it to the fax number Garret had. One of the changes was his direct permission was needed to speak to any LEOs or agencies. Not abnormal. I signed it and sent it back. It said the retainer and the bills would be paid by Garret but I was working for and would report to him and Garret simultaneously. I could include Evy in as well. He sent me a copy of my signed agreement with a note that anyone working on it would have to sign and date it as well.

A short while later we were all sitting around the conference room table. Cory at one point leaned her head on my shoulder as she was tired and I did not mind that at all. The perfume she wore was subtle and it mixed well with the scent of her skin. My thoughts began to go in that direction but then the Big G told me what he needed.

"We are being blackmailed."

I nodded and waited.

Evy continued. "I'm being threatened with dropping out of the race and they want a large sum of money."

"Any idea who 'they' is/are?" I asked.

"No."

"How are they communicating with you?"

"By email."

"Can I see the emails?" I asked.

They looked at each other. "Evy saw them and thought they were a prank and deleted them."

I shook my head. "Not good. I have several computer forensic experts at my disposal, so perhaps we can recover them."

"That's unlikely," said the Big G. "I am a programmer. I have a program that completely scrubs anything that is deleted. There are a lot of sensitive documents here."

"I can understand that, but from this point forward they have to be saved."

"Garrett had his people try to trace it and they couldn't."

I nodded. "Do you remember what it said?"

"Something about you have to pay for what you did. The damages come to 3 million dollars, something about that being a small sum for us, and then it said I had to drop out of the race."

A phone rang in one of the offices.

"That's the private line," Garrett said. He looked at me. "Excuse me for a minute."

I smiled and nodded.

"Any idea at all who this could be?"

"I get a lot of hate mail, emails, things like this. I want to save the planet and society, and people hate that."

I smiled.

"Or they hate the way you want to, or they hate themselves or they hate a million other possible things or some combination of those things. Or they see you as a genuine threat or they feel they have been injured by you, or none of the above or a million other possibilities." I paused and sipped some of the coffee. "At this point we don't have enough to go on to try to figure out motive."

Evy nodded. Garrett rejoined us and said to her, "Arthur Haskins, calling about the meet tomorrow."

"Okay," Evy said.

My eyebrows raised. Haskins was the Island's other Congressman. Congress person? Saying he was conservative was like saying the Sahara was a tad dry. Garrett noticed my expression.

"I know," he said. "We are diametrically opposed on most issues but there are a few things we agree on and we think people should cooperate on things they agree on."

"I agree completely," I said. And I did. But I noticed it was we and not she.

"So to the problem at hand is someone wants three million dollars and Evy to drop out of the race," I said. "If you deleted the only email how do you know it was for real?"

"We got a call, on our private line. They said that we didn't have a lot of time."

"They?"

"Well, it was a woman's voice but she kept using we, us, and things like that."

"What number did they call from?"

"It was private."

"Have you contacted the police, or the feds, or the police in DC?"

"No, we want to keep this private."

I nodded. "Was there any mention of what these alleged things you did were? Any truth to them?"

"No," Evy said.

"No to...?" I asked.

"No they didn't mention anything specifically and neither of us has done anything wrong."

"Except wanting social justice for all and saving our planet."

I had made turning a wince into a smile an art. I was willing to venture that no one on the entire planet did it as well as me. I inhaled and took a few seconds to mull things over.

"If the threat turns out to be genuine, and you

should for the sake of caution treat it as such for now, will you call the cops then? At least for security? I can't imagine the feds would want any harm coming to a member of congress."

"We would prefer to keep this whole thing private, and could you also do security if necessary?"

"Yes," I replied. "We are, however, because of the limited info available and in the event we do need security, talking about a lot of money here. I'm going to discount my rates for you because of Cory, but it'll still be a lot of hours."

Cory smiled at me; good thing I hadn't seen that earlier or I'd have ended up doing it for free.

"We appreciate that," Garrett said. "But as far as business goes please charge your normal rates. I have more than I could ever spend."

"Fair enough," I said. "Let me ask, are you concerned and do you feel you would want security now?"

"Well," Evy said, "I am afraid but I don't want people to notice the security, but I'd feel better." I noticed the "I".

"I can have people here with you. Tell them they are temps from an agency to help you, this way we have at least one guy here, and more if we need them. We can start with that and then if something makes it look more serious, we can call an expert in and make protection a more serious concern."

"You wouldn't do that yourself?" The Big G asked.

"I could, however I have access to some of the best people so I defer to people that know more than me. I have a retired Secret Service agent and they are acknowledged worldwide as being the best."

Garret nodded and Evy smiled. "This will also let me have someone here with an investigative background so that if something noteworthy happens, we jump on it. Can I have the number of your private line?"

"917-555-5309," Evy told me. I told them I also needed IP addresses, emails, and a plethora of other information. Garrett had become rich because of tech. We might be from different worlds but he was sharp. I had a paper in my hand to give to Eddie Martin.

"Okay, we can start with a twenty-five thousand dollar retainer. Twenty-five percent is non-refundable and we sadly need to charge you sales tax."

"No problem," Garrett said. "Would you prefer it to be wired? A check, credit card?"

"A check would be fine," I said.

"Whom do I make that out to?" he asked. "I" again.

He left the room shortly and returned with a check made out to Precision, my company. Before I put it in my wallet I noticed it was for double the amount I had asked. I looked at him.

"I appreciate your coming so fast. If there's more left over, we can probably keep you on retainer. If it goes past that, let me know."

"Fair enough," I said.

"I forgot if I mentioned it, but Todd, my martial arts instructor, is helping with security. I'd like for him to work with us. He is a dear friend."

"Shouldn't be a problem. You can use him as you see fit, but I'd ask for the sake of smooth running that he coordinate with me and listen if I make suggestions. I have the license, insurance, and bond, and if it hits the fan I'll get the heat, whether or not I deserve it."

"Absolutely," beamed the Big G.

We got up and left. I shook hands with both of them, left my card with my cell on it, told them I'd likely have someone there to them by mid-morning. I also told them if they were going to split up for a significant time period, they should if possible, let me know so I can have an op with each of them.

Cory kissed them both goodbye. She was a warm person but I noticed her goodbye to Evy was a little warmer than to Garrett. We left and Cory slipped her hand into mine as we walked to the car.

I asked her if she wanted me to take her home or to my place and she said her dad was okay tonight, her sister was around, and my place would be fine.

We got in through the door and she said hi to Molly. She turned and kissed me. One thing lead to another and I swept her up in my arms, ignored the pain in my shoulder and we went to bed.

We lay in bed after and she fell asleep. I enjoyed the warmth of her body and the scent of her skin. I hadn't been with anyone since Mandy. I felt some guilt. As much as I liked Cory and enjoyed being with her I missed Mandy. It had been about 2 weeks since I checked on Shane. I needed to do that. I had asked Smitty to take care of him. Smitty had taught me to use my hands when I was a kid, but so much more than that. He was doing well at Smitty's school. His dad, Mandy's ex-husband, whom I had liked, had also joined the adult class.

"Hey, you awake?" she asked very softly.

"I am, baby girl."

"Your shoulder okay?"

"Yeah."

"Want to sit up?"

"Sure, if you want to."

She did, and I followed suit. She got up and turned on the light on the nightstand on her side. She got a t-shirt I had folded on a chair that I would have put on before bed and got back under the covers.

"Hungry? Thirsty?"

She shook her head.

"Want to stay here or go downstairs?"

"Here's good," she said softly.

"TV on?"

She shook her head. "Can we talk a little?"

"Sure," I said.

"What do you think about Evy and Garrett?"

"Think as far as?"

"Well, firstly their problem and secondly just them in general. I know you probably don't agree with her positions."

"I wish they hadn't deleted that email. I'll help them if I can. It's so early on, I don't know if I can or if this isn't just a hoax."

"What do you think of them? As people, I mean?"

"I don't really know them well enough to form an opinion. Why don't you tell me about them a little?"

"She was a friend in high school and college. She was looking for a job and working as a waitress at the diner on Victory Boulevard. She was approached by this group about running for office. She did a year in the service overseas about a year after high school graduation. That would help pay for college and she figured it would help with running for office. She tried to run for City Council but it was a disaster. She didn't get enough signatures and the whole campaign was a mess. Garrett was a member of that group. They started dating and she got elected to Congress. He ran the campaign that time."

"So you know her well?"

"We went out a while," she said, watching me as she told me.

I nodded.

"Does that bother you?"

"That you had a relationship with her? Or that you're bi?"

She laughed. "Either."

"No. Neither has anything to do with me. I enjoy being with you."

"It would bother some people."

"Some people are idiots."

"Hell yes," she said.

"I believe that whatever two consenting adults do, consent being an important part, is their business. If it doesn't hurt someone else."

She smiled again. "She told me early on that she only really liked girls. She's a good person and I love her. It took a while for us to be friends because I broke it off and she was hurt. I told her that I had relationships with men and that I enjoyed being with them and she kept trying to convince me I was lying to myself."

"Judging by the way you cried out and your body shook about a half hour ago, I'd say she was wrong," I smiled.

She pushed me a little and laughed again. I really did like her laugh.

"She means well but she has these really far out views. We had a professor in college and she idolized her. She was a member of some crazy group and she called people in the Weather Underground heroes and wore a Che Guevara shirt. I have some Cuban in me, and my dad had told us about the horrors of what Castro did. I tried telling Evy this but she never listened."

"Wow, a Che Guevara shirt. Maybe that's what she wore when her Hitler shirt was in the laundry. I wonder if she knew that Che killed gays?"

"Yeah, like that. Evy is, I want to say, book smart but she remembers things well that she learned in class, but she didn't think a lot for herself. This whole thing, her getting elected and Garrett, it's..." She searched for the right word.

"Strange?" I offered.

"Yeah."

"Tell me about him."

"He is always nice, but we don't know much about him. He has a lot of money. I mean a lot. And his friends...there was so much money in her campaign. She couldn't find a campaign headquarters, so he bought the building. He wrote a check for it, didn't even bother with a title search."

"That is a lot of money."

"But there just seems to be something about him. I can't say what. It's always us, we, you know?"

"Except when it comes to his money, right?"

"Yeah. You noticed that?"

I nodded.

"It could just be he doesn't do well with people or he has something like Asperger's."

"I thought about that. My cousin is like that. Amazing girl, she just has trouble with certain situations. But with him, I don't think so. I would bet anything he thinks he bought you tonight."

I chuckled. "That he didn't. But you're right. He thinks he did." I reached over and grabbed my phone. Tony Medaglia responded to the text I sent him earlier. He'd be at my office at 8:30 A.M. and Evy's campaign after. He was a retired cop, narcotics, won the Mr. New York's Finest Body Building contest. Even tempered and formidable yet not overbearing. I'd get someone else to handle nights for them tomorrow. I sent a text to Chief Mariano. He had mentioned he had a friend that had retired recently and was looking for work. I told him I had a job and that if he thought his friend might be interested to have them call or text me in the A.M.

"I feel a little guilty sometimes. She went into the service after we broke up. She told me she still loves me."

"If she's gay like she says why is she with Garrett?"

"I've asked that. She doesn't answer."

I nodded. "And how do you feel about it?"

"I love her as a friend. I liked the physical part with her but we didn't really connect otherwise, not like lovers do."

I nodded and we were quiet for a while.

"I noticed you didn't seem enthusiastic about Todd," I said after a time.

"Be careful of him," Cory said to me seriously. "He likes hurting people, and Garrett likes having him around."

"Oh?"

"Yeah, he hurt some protester a while back. Garrett spent a lot of money keeping it out of the papers."

"Listen, we have a group. We get together at The Cargo Café once a week but once a month we have a formal discussion. Evy used to go but not anymore. We have been doing it since college. It's my turn next. I can bring someone to talk with the group about what they do and then they take questions. Would you be interested?"

"Um, sure, if you wanted me to. I'm not sure how interesting I'd be."

"You're plenty interesting," she said.

"Okay, if you want me to," I said. "You know, it's very common in my profession to give a person that refers a job a referral fee. You just got me a fifty-thousand-dollar retainer. I'd like you to take a fee from me. It's standard, normal."

"I could never take money from you," she said. "Please don't ask me to."

"Honey, are you sure?"

"Yes, just do one thing for me."

"Tell me."

"Make sure Evy is okay."

"I will."

She ran her hand over my chest and below the covers. I pulled her to me and we kissed, gently at first. She slid on top of me, and she whispered in my ear, "I can think of a better way to pay my fee," she said.

Turns out it was a fee I didn't mind paying.

6

CORY HAD LEFT WELL after midnight. I felt good, which was why I think I started feeling bad. I felt guilty, like I had betrayed Mandy. That made no sense. She'd want me to be happy. If I had moved faster, if I had my gun instead of it being across the room. My thoughts turned to Stanton. For months now I'd remember killing him when I felt like this. That deep sadness and despair that I was never going to see her again. I carried no guilt about killing Stanton. If I could, I'd kill him again. My hatred for him was like a band aid for the grief I felt.

I knew Jack Harmon was working nights for a while so I sent him a text message and he answered back. He'd get back to his office about 3PM and he'd have an hour. I told him I'd see him then and I'd bring coffee.

I sept uneasily. I dreamed about Mandy dying, and killing Stanton. I woke up three or four times, found myself wishing Cory had stayed, and then felt guilty about that. I was up at six, looked bad, and felt worse. After stretching, push-ups, and core exercises I discarded the idea of working out. I could hear the scar tissue popping in my shoulder as I did the sixty pushups. I added five a week and in less than two months I'd be back to a hundred.

I took care of Molly and the cat, headed to the office, and met Tony Medaglia. We had coffee and caught up. His wife and kids were all well. I hadn't seen him since the wake. I briefed him on everything.

"So I am there to make sure it's safe, watch this guy Todd, and employ my considerable investigative prowess in the event we get contacted by the blackmailer?"

"Yes."

"It's a good thing leaping over tall buildings in a single bound is your department."

"I'm not leaping over even moderate buildings these days."

He smiled. "You doing okay?"

"Yeah. You know how it is, some good days, more bad. Same thing running around in my head. I'm either thinking about losing her or killing him."

He nodded.

"It won't bring her back but it's still fun to do."

"You did the world a fucking favor," my friend told me.

"Yeah. But I probably spend too much time thinking."

He nodded. "Need anything?"

Yeah, I need her back, I thought. "Just a new shoulder, pal," I said.

"Hell, if you find one send a couple to me."

He got up to go. "Keep in touch. Something on the whole isn't right here."

"Wouldn't be the first time a client lied to us," I offered.

"Or the last."

I walked him out and he left through the back door. When I went back into my office I noticed my reflection in the bar over the mirror. I had a headache and my face was drawn and the lack of sleep was evident. I grabbed the bottle of Jameson and put a double shot in the coffee on my desk. I swallowed four aspirins, drinking most of the Irish Coffee in two swallows. Shoulder felt good so no need for anything stronger in the pill department.

Jeff got in shortly and it was a fairly busy morning. We caught a homicide case from Tim Parlatore's office. He was in Hawaii on a federal case but we spoke with the attorney that was handling it until he got back in a day or so. Ordinarily I'd handle that but with the blackmail case, Jeff suggested John Donohue. John was one of the first guys that broke me in. He ran security for the Knicks for years and had just retired. He was free and agreed to handle it. Tom came by and picked up a couple of surveillance cases we had. Jeff noticed I was tired. We had a few interviews with some new investigators and he offered to handle them and I accepted. I went outside to catch some air and to figure out what the hell I would do until I met with Jack at three. I noticed both Bruno and Danielle were sitting on the block. I remembered catching Burtone and Sullivan following Mandy. They were sitting too close of course. I leaned on the building facing away from them and saw Cory had sent me a text. I told her I was going to go home and asked if she wanted to drop by. She said she'd be there. I decided to lose my shadows. That wasn't too hard. I parked my car about a few blocks away from my home. Unlikely they would even look if they passed by the house.

I had some problems I had to take care of. I had to figure out what to do about Bruno and Danielle. I was meeting Harmon and had to start chipping away at a fifty-thousand-dollar retainer. I had to put things in place to find out who was blackmailing my client and why. I felt weak and tired. I'd prefer anger. Maybe punching through Bruno's windshield. I felt like I hadn't slept in a week. I walked the short distance and went in, leaving the front door unlocked. I fell asleep on the couch looking at the picture of Mandy I had in the living room. I was dimly aware of Cory coming in and she came and sat by me. Apparently I had been weeping again as I slept. She reached over and brushed tears away from my face. I was still so tired. I laid my head in her lap and fell asleep again.

I woke up at one and she hadn't moved. She rested her hand gently on my back. I woke up and she had made us lunch. I'd had a few chicken breasts in the fridge and she did a great job with it and vegetables and brown rice. We ate and talked at the kitchen table.

"I need you to know, I enjoy being with you very much. You've come to mean a lot to me in a very short period of time. I'm happy when I see you. I also feel guilty. I shouldn't. She wouldn't want me to. It has nothing to do with you."

She nodded. Her face was sad. "You feel responsible for her death."

I nodded.

"You know that you shouldn't, but you do?"

"Yeah," I said.

We ate in silence for a while but it was not an uncomfortable silence. She was wearing jeans and a t-shirt and she looked amazing.

"I kind of pushed the grief back. I let my anger, my rage about Stanton dominate what I felt. It caught up with me."

She nodded. "Do you feel bad about killing him?"

"The truth?"

She nodded.

"No. If I could, I'd kill him again. He got off too easy. It was self-defense, he shot at us, but I'd have killed him anyway for taking her from me. From her son. I'd make him pay for my pain. He had killed my friend Vickie. He was a cancer."

She nodded. "I'm sorry if that is disturbing," I said.

"It's not sweetheart. I'm so sorry it happened. I wish I could help."

I put my fork down, got up, and walked around the table. I bent down and gently raised her chin and kissed her. She held my face and kissed me back.

"You do help," I told her.

———

At three I strode into the *Staten Island Times* with a dozen donuts and pastries from a real Italian bakery, and two gourmet dark roast coffees. I stopped for a minute and spoke with Frank Donnelly, who in my opinion was one the last real crime reporters, along with Jack Harmon. I had given him an interview on a criminal case I was handling last week and we talked a bit and he grabbed one of the donuts and headed off to a shooting.

A couple of minutes later I was at Harmon's desk and we sipped the coffee. We each grabbed two of the donuts and he put the rest in the break room at my request so I didn't swallow them whole.

"So in return for hurdling me towards diabetes," Harmon said. "What can I do you for?"

"Tell me about my clients."

"Ahhhhhhh. Lying to you?"

"Not telling me anything."

"Very little is known about Garrett, I can tell you this. He came from money but he made tons himself. He formed a Super Pac and they sent millions to the Sanders campaign. I knew a guy he was a reporter at the *City Herald*. He was covering a story involving some guy that works for him, hired muscle from what I understand. He roughed up someone. The article never got written, the kid I knew sold his goddamned soul, and he works for The Big G as we speak. He got a fifty thousand dollar signing bonus."

"I heard something about that," I said.

"I covered a few press conferences with them. She quickly became a politician, the usual— lots of talk no substance. She has a rough road ahead of her. She portrayed herself as middle of the road and managed to get in. Even with the money behind her it's going to be a tough one."

"A politician who lies...stop the presses. So give me your impression of her."

"Hard to say. Look, I'm a blue dog dem, a Kennedy man. That's why we manage to agree on some things. She can believe what she wants but she comes off..."

As I waited while he searched for the word, the second donut met its fate. I noticed a reporter I knew walk by with Leticia Remauro, who was apparently being interviewed. They both waved and I waved back.

"Hollow," Harmon finished.

I nodded. "What about the hired muscle? Todd, I believe is his name."

"He hurt some guy more than he had to. That was what the guy I knew believed."

"Well if it was you that story would have been written."

"Yeah, and I'll die poor."

"Better poor than a whore," I said. "The way it is, pal, 99 percent of what is said to be news is commentary and both sides believe only the other side is fake news. If you don't keep doing what you do it'll be that much worse."

"Well, it's not like I can sing or dance."

"Well you can, but ain't nobody going to pay to see that."

We laughed.

"Can you make a few discreet inquiries for me?"

"Anything you can share?"

"Not yet. Truth is I don't know if there will be, but if there is, it's yours."

"Am I still on the Holiday Party at Peter Luger list?"

I smiled. "Hell yes."

"Let me know if you find anything else out, and I will find out what I can," Jack told me.

I got a text from Tony Medaglia. "All is well. Lots of enthusiasm here. Todd is interesting. He obviously disapproves of us and seems to get angry quickly."

"Angry at you?" I texted back.

"Nope. The world."

"I'll be headed in your direction in the morning," I sent him.

Jeff sent me a text that he had arranged security for Garrett and Evy tonight and he was going home. He also let me know that Eddie Martin had come in and was waiting for me. He still hadn't grasped that when he sent text messages he didn't have to start it with "Hey it's Jeff" and then at the end say "Goodbye." I smiled and replied thanks, I'd see him in the morning. I also texted him "Jeff it's a text you don't have to say good bye." I texted Tony I'd be stopping by in a few. Jeff texted me back "Okay goodbye"

I got in the car and hit the radio. Yes greeted me with "Love Will Find A Way." Although many fans thought it was blasphemy, I thought Trevor Rabin made the band.

I went back to the office and a short while later was sitting with Eddie. I gave him an envelope with ten thousand dollars in it. He might accomplish what I needed for that, or he might need more, but odds are, he'd accomplish it.

I gave him Evy's email address and the email address that sent the emails, the IP address at the campaign headquarters, street address, private phone number, and anything else I could think of.

"Triton?"

"Yeah. I've been wondering about the significance of that."

The email address was triton19 and it was a secured .net email address. It was a free service that provided encryption and made it more difficult to find out who went back to an email address.

"Well it is one of Neptune's moons. It is significant because it's the only moon known to orbit in retrograde," I said. "More than likely it is a Kuiper belt object that was caught in Neptune's gravity. Also the son of Poseidon."

Eddie laughed mirthfully. "Very good, Jimmy!" I smiled because he praised me the same way I'd heard him praise his son. I'm smart, but Eddie was Einstein. If he was a PI he'd be Nero Wolfe and I'd be Archie. We never spoke of it but my recall is exceptional. His went beyond that. He likely had an eidetic memory.

"Two other meanings for the word and you win the bonus. Any ideas?"

"Not in the slightest, pal."

"A particle with one proton and two neutrons, the nucleus of a tritium atom."

"And the other?" I asked.

"A type of warm water mollusk with a kind of ornate shell."

"Interesting," I said. It was, but it also gave insight into Eddie. He'd use that knowledge as information came back in regard to his inquiries and it might help him determine the identity of whoever it was that sent the email.

"What do you want specifically?" he asked me.

"Well, if it had been a few days ago, everything you can tell about who it was. Now though, I'd just like a way to contact them."

He was quiet for a moment. His eyes closed and he sat there. He could be there thirty seconds or thirty minutes. I did something similar to that but my eyes always stayed open. He was working things out.

"What about having them contact you?"

"Sure, you can even let them know I won't try to find out who they are. I want to talk and meet and see about helping them accomplish their goals, in a manner of speaking."

"Okay," he said and I left.

Cory had messaged me a bunch of hearts and told me her dad was doing better and that she was going to be with him tonight and asked if we could see each other tomorrow. I cut and pasted the hearts and added "Hell Yes!" and went home.

I was almost to the end of the recovery. Well, the recovery for the physical wounds. Most of the preceding months were a blur. Doctor visits. PT. Working out on my own. Work mixed in between. Only a few things stuck out.

There was a night in late fall when I felt anger. Mostly I felt weak. It sometimes took a pot of coffee for me to go to PT or to work out. I wanted to be alone but I missed being around people. I had been warned that the shoulder would heal over time, and strenuous activity was frowned on.

"Listen, you stubborn fuck," Doctor Shur said to me in his thick accent and he waited to make sure our eyes met. "You will come back from this. There will be pain but you're strong. It will heal, and you'll be almost good as new. Don't fuck it up. Be a good boy, Jimmy, and don't do something stupid because you have a hole in your heart."

"Ok, Doc."

His voice got softer. "I know what you're going through. I lost a woman to violence. I know despair and pain. Don't fuck yourself up and end up without an arm. She wouldn't want that for you."

I nodded.

I actually talked to him in my head. "Well let's see how good a job you did, Doc," I said to the air.

I went to Duffy's. The middle of the bar was crowded; both ends were sparse. There were a lot of people at the tables. I sat by the end of the bar closest to Forest Avenue. It might feel good to hit someone that deserved it. Kevin, the bartender, asked me what I was having. I asked for a shot of Jack and a draft. They had Bluepoint Blueberry Ale on draft. It was not at all sweet and it was absurdly good. There was a prime candidate for the main event opposite me. Military guy, maybe. Big, strong, about my age. Staring at the bar that was between his forearms. I looked around the room. I knew a few people here and there. There was a woman, slender but curvy with a beautiful face, and she was swaying a little. A guy that had been with a crowd sat next to her. She had no idea he was there. I realized I didn't want a fight. I wanted someone to hit me. I wondered if I might feel like I was real again. I downed two shots and a draft right away but it turns out I didn't have the taste for it. "The Marine" as I came to call him glanced once in a while around the room. Our eyes met and he nodded. I nodded back. His eyes came to rest on the slender woman and her suitor. He took her by the arm and he tried to get her to leave. She shook her head and pulled away. She was very drunk. I edged a little closer and caught Kevin's attention and nodded my head toward them. He watched for a second and came over.

"He know her?" I asked.

"No," Kevin said.

"Know her?"

"No, other than she was in here a four or five times. She left with a guy once."

"Does it look like she wants this clown's company?"

"Nope."

"I'm not going to let him take her out of here."

"I agree," Kevin said.

Some of the suitor's friends came over and they tried to get the woman to go with them. She shook her head and said in a slightly slurred voice, "No, I'm fine here, thank you."

I removed my keys and my phone. I hadn't brought my gun. I slipped the leather coat off and hung it around the back of my chair. I was about two steps away when the Marine appeared in the middle of the group.

"She doesn't want to go with you guys."

"Who the fuck asked you?" the suitor asked in what he likely thought was a menacing tone.

"I did," I said. The group turned in my direction.

"And who the fuck are you?"

"Will the answer to that question actually help you?"

"What?"

"Is knowing who I am actually going to help you? Or would the fact that I could drive your teeth out the back of your head be of more use?"

There were four of them. None a real physical specimen. The girl, through her haze, looked at me for the first time. She smiled but she was sad. Her eyes were a little teary.

"Miss, what's your name?"

"Eileen."

"Do you want to go anywhere with these men, Eileen," the Marine asked her.

She shook her head. "No."

"There it is, fellas. She's not going anywhere. If you object, we can get to it here or go out in the parking lot and not ruin Duff's bar," I said. "Make your play, and let's get to it."

They all looked at each other and the message seeped through that the odds were not in their favor. They grumbled and tossed a few insults our way. I let that go. Always give them an out. If calling me an asshole saved face for their friends, it's better than me in the precinct all night after putting some of them in the hospital. The Marine stayed by the girl. I hadn't seen Kevin pick up a small club he kept behind the bar, but I saw him put it back on one of the shelves. I don't know what the hell it was. It looked like a cross between a bowling pin and a rolling pin.

The bar had cleared away a little. The Marine looked at me and I gestured to one of the seats near mine. He nodded and walked toward me, hand extended.

"Henry Stokes."

"Jonathan Creed," I said, grasping his hand.

He sat by me on the empty stool facing the mirror behind the bar and I sat at the end. We were both at the corner and could see each other. Kevin brought us a couple of drafts and a couple of shots of Jack. Apparently Henry was a man of good taste. Eileen watched us and after a few seconds she made her way over and sat next to Henry. Kevin looked at her and she asked him for coffee in a soft voice.

"I'm sorry," she said. "I'm sorry I caused you so much trouble."

"You didn't, Miss," I said.

"I don't know what would have happened if they got me outside," she said.

"Kevin wouldn't have let them do that," I said.

We were quiet for a while. I put the shot away and half of the draft. Henry sat and stared at the bar. I couldn't tell how far along he was. No visible signs.

"Funny," I mused. "I wouldn't have minded a fight."

"Me, either," Henry admitted. "Not a good day."

"Same here," I said.

"Me, too," Eileen added. "About the bad day, I mean. Not the fight."

I chuckled and Henry smiled. First time I saw any real emotion from him.

"May I ask," Eileen queried toward me.

I took a deep breath. "My fiancée was murdered not long ago," I shared. That was a bit uncharacteristic of me. I drank another swallow of the draft. I told them an abbreviated version.

"Oh my God," she said. "My boss knows you. He's a lawyer right around the corner. I'm so sorry."

"Thank you." I paused. "Why are you upset?"

"My daughter. She won't speak to me. I went through a bad divorce." She paused a second. "I caught my husband sexually abusing my daughter. It was years in court, I had to work to pay legal fees. I dropped out of college. I have loans I can't pay. My mother raised my daughter while I worked, and hell, she did such a great job with me I ended up with a child molester but there was no other choice. I had to declare bankruptcy twice. I finally won. He never saw her but my mother did damage to my daughter. I should have been there for her."

"It seems to me you did the best you possibly could," Henry told her.

"She won't even talk to me. She blames me for her childhood and she's right." She sipped her coffee, tears running down her face.

"There's a chance she might realize how things were," I said.

"And if she doesn't?" Eileen asked me. Her eyes searched mine. Full of pain, and she was tired. The kind of tired that grief caused.

"Then you know that you did the absolute best you could for her. And that's all you could do," I said. "All you can do is the best you can do. My bet is one day she understands that."

We were quiet a bit. Kevin refilled my draft. He took the shot glass and looked at me. I shook my head. Eileen dried her eyes with a napkin.

We both looked at Henry.

"I was overseas. In Afghanistan. Second tour. There was this guy. Big Charlie. Dopey kid from out west. Was with us from basic training. He had no family, at least none he cared to talk about. He had left home and joined the service as fast as he could because of his life at home. His father beat him with a belt once a day whether he needed it or not, he used to say. He attached himself to me. He was annoying sometimes but he was a good kid. Do anything for you. We were ambushed and I fell. Hit the ground hard, did something to my leg. The kid ran to me and carried me out. Saved my life. We had about two weeks left to go."

He downed his shot of Jack with no visible effect. He kept staring at the patch of bar between his arms. "Roadside bomb hit us. Charlie was in the vehicle in front of me. He was trapped. No way to get him out. His Hummer caught fire. Everyone else got out but he couldn't. We got the fire suppressed. We called for help. It was twenty minutes away. The fire started up again and we couldn't stop it. I got burned trying to pull him out. He started screaming for me. For me to help him. He begged me. We couldn't get him out."

I was quiet and I watched his face. He wasn't in the bar anymore. Eileen was crying for him. He didn't see us. He just stared at that small patch of bar.

"When he realized we couldn't get him out, he begged me to shoot him. He kept saying don't let me burn, Hank, please. Black smoke everywhere, the smell of the vehicle and my friend burning. I shot him. I killed my friend." Tears dropped on that patch of bar now. "I shot my friend," he said again. "Three years ago today." Eileen slid over to him and hugged him, crying. I reached over and squeezed his hand.

"I'm sorry," I said.

He nodded. I took out two of my business cards and gave them to both of them. I took out two hundred and put it on the bar. I told Kevin to keep the change and I took out another hundred and told him to make sure he got them a cab and that they both got home safe.

I said goodnight to them and left. I walked outside, and the air was cold and clear. It had that clean smell when a cold front comes in, and the sky was bright. No moon but a lot of stars. I looked up at the sky as I walked towards my car. It was like the sky had been cleaned, like Windex across a dirty window. The stars alone lit it up.

It was like taking a trash can overflowing with garbage,

I thought, *and ramming a lid down on it and then polishing the outside and selling it as art.*

"If you are up there, you should be sued for malpractice," I said to the sky. "Hell, I'll serve you with the papers when I get there." I got to the car and opened it and looked up at the sky once more. "Why did you take her?"

I fell asleep wondering what had happened to them. I hoped maybe something would happen between them; the world had certainly taken from them. I didn't feel better knowing other people were hurting. It did remind me that I wasn't the only one.

PART II

―――――――

"I think the thing I've wanted most
was just never meant to be.
A thousand waves, a thousand ghosts.
Their sorrows follow me."

"The Water Lets You In"
Book of Fears

7

I HAD a lot to think about and took my time Wednesday morning. Tony was inside the campaign headquarters when I got there at ten-thirty in a small room to the left of the reception area. There were a lot of people coming and going. He had a clear view of everyone that came in or out. The receptionist asked me how she could help. I smiled and told her I was here to see Tony and pointed to the room. She smiled and nodded.

As I walked toward the room a guy who I shrewdly guessed to be Todd came out of the door leading to the back rooms. He moved quickly towards me and put himself in my way.

"Can I help you?"

"It doesn't look like you're up to that task, kid, but I'll let you know if I need a tire changed."

He was about my height and heavier by a solid twenty pounds. I ran between 240 and 250 and it wasn't a common occurrence for someone my height to be bigger. It was hard muscle, and that was even less common occurrence. He had blond dyed hair cut short and spiked and stylish. Well, what passes for style. He was late twenties or early thirties. I personally thought he looked like he had a shark fin on his cranium or that his hair had been wet and he stuck a fork in a wall socket. He had sunglasses on the top of his head, Ray Bans, apparently. At least he wasn't wearing them inside. He was clean shaven with a square jaw that sat on top a 21-inch neck. His face went red immediately and his left leg dropped back and his hands started to raise. A southpaw.

"He's okay, Todd. He's my boss." Tony had gotten there quickly.

Todd was evidently unimpressed. He glared at me and I smiled back.

"I don't like his sense of humor," he snapped.

"I could try and explain it to you, kid, if you want."

Todd's face got redder. Tony rolled his eyes. I smiled. We stood like that for a few seconds and Garrett came through the door.

"Oh, I'm glad you guys met. Jonathan, can I have a word?"

"Sure thing, Garrett," I said.

He turned and I told Tony I'd be back. I winked at Todd who eyed me coldly now. We made our way back to Garrett's office. I heard Evy on the phone with someone as I walked past a closed door. He opened the door and went in first. I followed as befitting my social status. He had a bar that was bigger and better stocked than mine with an array of single malt scotches. I saw he also kept some good ports.

"It's almost five somewhere," he said. "Care for something?"

"I am rather partial to Broadbent Port," I said.

"You have good taste."

"Thank you," I replied. He poured from the decanter and not the bottle that said Broadbent Vintage Port. He had actual port glasses. Fancy for a temporary election headquarters. I sat with my glass and sipped it and it was superb.

"Anything for me yet?" he asked.

"We just started. This is going to take some time. There's not a lot to go on."

He nodded.

"Anything new on your end?"

"Not so far." Now I nodded. "Garrett, do you have any idea who would do this? I don't even know yet if you are the target or just Evy or both. Is there anything you can give me, someplace I can look?"

He pursed his lips and thought for a minute. I looked at some of the pictures he had on the wall. Vacation pics, martial arts training, and him with famous people.

"It has to be establishment GOP. She's a threat to them."

"This is Staten Island, Garrett, not the deep South, pre-civil rights. Most of the pubs here are moderate, very much like Blue Dog Dems."

"That isn't moderate anymore, Jonathan." I raised my eyebrows. "We view people like that that call themselves democrat as being part of the problem."

"That's a bit extreme. It is a million miles away from what she campaigned on," I said.

"If they can lie so can we."

"My point is, though, you are more likely to have them vote her out than to threaten her."

"I wouldn't be too sure," Garrett said. "The people in

this country that have held power are terrified it is slipping away."

Please, God, let me go through this retainer as fast as I can, I thought.

"Well, we are likely going to have little time until they make their next move," I said.

He nodded.

"One more thing," I said. "I know Todd is a friend of yours but he failed the door test."

"The door test?"

"When I ran security at clubs I would always have the guy that manned the door tested. It's important the front man keeps cool. He is the key because he decides who is let inside. But you also don't want him killing business. Todd gets angry quickly. He should ease up a bit."

"Oh, I see. I will talk with him about that."

"Good."

I declined another glass of port regretfully because the conversation would have soured the drink. I passed the room where Evy was and I heard her voice still. I walked past a bunch of people and didn't see the Toddster anywhere. Tony and I walked outside.

"Well, what do you think?" I asked him.

"You pay well, Jimmy, but I should charge you extra for the nauseating rhetoric I am subjected to."

"Look at it this way, pal, you are disproving socialism by accepting compensation forty percent above industry standard."

"Yeah, I meant to ask you about that, boss. That's a lot of money, rhetoric or no."

"I'm still making a ton on you, pal, don't worry."

A car started and I looked in that direction. In a few

minutes the car pulled out did a broken U and went the other way. An old Toyota with dark windows. It needed a muffler.

"Where is the Toddster?"

"He had something to do for Evy, an errand or something. He looked less than pleased. I'll say this, boss, I watched him and he has that same coiled up energy you do. He actually has a few pounds on you. I know you're good but if it came down to it and I was you, I'd shoot him. If I was ringside, I'd put my money on you but it may not be easy. It's also a pretty safe bet he doesn't like you."

"Well, I didn't just annoy him for the sake of it, although it was fun."

"See if he kept his cool?"

"Yup," I said.

"He failed that test."

"Yup."

"He'd just love it if he heard you call him the Toddster."

"Well we shall see if the opportunity comes up."

"Did you see the videos of him on YouTube?"

"YouTube?" I asked. "Trendy bastard."

"Nope, it would be TikTok if I was trendy." He pulled his phone out and showed me. There were several videos, one of an MMA fight, one of him training and teaching if you want to call it that.

"Can you send it to me?"

He looked down at his phone for a bit and then replied with, "Done. Remember the evil karate teacher in *The Karate Kid*? The No Mercy guy?"

"Sure."

"It's him on steroids. I mean that literally and figuratively. I did the bodybuilding circuit for years, so I know juicing. No one is that strong and has that much endurance without chemical assistance. He'd place in a power lifting contest in his weight class."

"So I am assuming you don't mean like a few hundred cc's of tess replacement every two weeks?"

"Hell no, everyone over thirty should do that. I'm talking Anadrol 50 in mega doses."

I whistled.

"What's your best bench ever at what weight?"

"Straight 405 raw, legit pause. I weighed about 245."

"Impressive, boss. I'll bet you're not far off that."

"About 30, 40 pounds."

"You'd be doing 6 after a year of Anadrol. And he's mean, like I said. He likes hurting people."

"Sadly, pal, we ain't in a business where we can let people scare us off."

He laughed. "I fucking knew you'd say that or something like that. We need to go for cocktails, soon. But be careful, boss. I don't like this whole thing, and I like him least of all."

I nodded.

"I know you're good, Jimmy. I seen you move, but remember he's up there and he is absolutely brutal, vicious. He likes hurting people, you don't. And he's strong, really strong."

"I can make an exception in his case, as far as hurting people goes. And, I shall endeavor to utilize my intellect if I need to thwart him."

"You'll hit him with a book?"

"My laptop."

He snickered. I said goodbye and headed to the office.

I got a text message from Mary, our receptionist. Tim Parlatore called and he'd call me on the cell later tonight. He told her he'd be around the Island later in the week and was hoping we could get together. Been a while since I saw him. I was fortunate that I liked most of my clients. Many like Tim were friends. He gave us a steady stream of work, which I appreciated.

I had a feeling about Todd. Cory had messaged me she'd be at the campaign headquarters that afternoon and asked if we could hook up. I told her to text me before she left there and we would figure out where.

I went to the office and found Truck sitting on the block. He was solo again or the girl had switched cars and gotten better. He was actually further down the block but that was likely because there were few spots on the street.

Jeff and I kicked that problem around a few hours. Lunch didn't help the creative thought process. Tony called me and checked in and we had updates on the other cases. I told him I might be back later and we had Jimmy Hannan coming in for night duty. The power couple was going to be together for the night. Tony mentioned Todd had been given some kind of secret assignment and he hadn't been back. When Tony had asked Garrett he just said he was on something for the campaign and was evasive. I told him to keep an eye out for Cory as she would be there later.

"Jimmy, hang on a minute," he said. "I may have something, boss, in regard to a suspect. We got an email."

"Do the clients know?"

"Yes, I have a copy and all that computer info that comes with it for a tech guy. I'm holding on to a copy for you. Garrett also told me over the next few days they are going to be splitting up a bunch of times, and besides Todd and me, they are going to need more coverage. Todd, it looks like, will stay with Garrett."

"What does the email say?"

"Pay what you owe, a million dollars. Tell that bitch to drop out."

"Okay, let them know I know and I have someone working on it."

"I have the impression he is going to also," Tony said.

"T, use that wit and charm of yours to dissuade him. Tell him I got someone doing it and it could cause problems if they criss cross each other."

"I'll do my best. Did you see those videos I sent you?"

"I didn't, pal, but I will. Keep an eye on things. See you soon. I need to get a problem out of my hair so I free up."

"Done," he said.

I am good at what I do. I've kept people out of prison that should have gone, which I did provided they didn't hurt children. Those people were on their own. I have solved problems and gotten people out of situations. Most of the time I won. Getting my fiancé killed was one of the rare times I was unsuccessful. Yes, I was good and I was arrogant enough to know that, but I also knew the reason I was so good. My greatest ability was selecting the people I worked with. They were the best. They were the primary reason I accomplished what people hired me to so often. Tony was no exception.

I had hired him when I first started out and sadly the work declined when we lost a major client. We had lost the client, an insurance company, because the new claims manager had a "relationship" with another PI company. She got moved to another state after a year when her numbers and losses went through the roof and it turned out that company was sending PIs from Buffalo, eight hours away to do the same work my people were and not as well. I lost Tony; he went to work for a hospital running security and he did well. Eventually, he retired from it and found me again. I remembered the decline of my work product when he left initially and happily brought him back on board. He was shortly going to solve my case for me.

Eddie Martin called me over the intercom, and when I poked my head in the door he also told me about the email. I couldn't help smiling because he was giving me that info exactly when I figured he would. Anyone that didn't believe in magic, didn't know Eddie. He said he had something to work on now.

Mary let me know over the intercom that I had two visitors and after I gave the okay she brought them down to my office on her way out to lunch. It wasn't a surprise to me to see both of them together, but it would be to some.

It was very rare for anyone, regardless of party, that was elected to office to get into said office without people like them. It was part of the system and would go on with or without my approval. I had sometimes worked for them or people that they referred to me. People knew me and knew my rules. They had used me enough to know what I would and would not do. There had been occasion where I had gone to them for information or introduction and once, Bobby had worked for me. He handled a job I did in DC that required someone with more of a background in the bowels of politics than an investigator.

Bobby had spent his life working for the highest bidder on both sides, although in reality he was a conservative with a few liberal streaks. Working for a public utilities corporation he was elected to a union position and he brutalized the company people in negotiations. When he began to irritate upper management to the point every time they lost position his name was behind it, they offered him a position and then he did his job and brutalized the union. He made his living by winning fights. If there had ever been the possibility of full contact chess, beyond the musings of George Carlin, he'd have been the world champ. Politics was warfare. He was general. A Hessian general.

Frank was more an enigma. Anyone with any fantasy that people that ran under a party banner would adhere to principle ahead of profit, election or re-election, would have their world collapse if they had a five-minute conversation with him. The majority of those in politics were there because they meant to rule. Most were sociopathic litmus paper and they would turn color in accord to what solution they were dipped in, and Frank knew it. There are examples everywhere of people belonging to a party embracing a position clearly at odds with the philosophy of the party for gain or advantage. All you had to do was open a newspaper.

Frank would back people in either party. He brought coin, contacts, and more to a candidate. But he was consistent. The people he backed made small business a platform issue. He had money, more than most, but how much more no one had any idea. Some people said his nose bent one way. You weren't successful in the construction business in New York if you didn't have contacts on both sides, but I didn't read him that way. On the surface he was kind and even tempered, but if you had the eye for it, you'd know there were gale force winds underneath the gentle breeze. I saw it, but it's not hard to recognize what's in you, in others. He'd been around the block enough times that he'd have left a trench in the concrete where he'd walked that would have hit ground water.

Neither had the money of the influence of someone like Garrett, but the Big G would inevitably reach out to people like them. And although having more money than the GDP of some countries was formidable, if Garrett wanted dirty work done he'd have to have some of his people call people who would call people and so on to get it done. Frank would be having breakfast with people that would be at the end of that chain. Or he might be at the end of that chain himself.

Over the years, respect between us had become friendship. I could trust them. That might surprise a lot of people. It started out that they kept their word. They did what they said they would do. There were people I knew longer, that I liked. But I wouldn't trust them as far as I could throw them, though I could throw them farther than most. Know people for what they are and have no illusions about that. I knew a lot of so called "bad guys" who could be counted on to keep their word and do what they said they would, and I had known more than one prosecutor who would do the opposite of what they said the moment you were out the door. You can co-exist with a predator as long as you don't forget that when it sees you, it sees food. I remembered both of them had come to Mandy's wake but not together if memory served.

They sat and I asked if they would care for coffee or something else, which they both politely declined.

"To what do I owe a visit from the Wise Men? Business or pleasure?"

Frank chuckled and Bobby smiled. "We came here because we were recommended you for a job, although you may have gotten it anyway," Bobby said.

"Although your client was relieved to hear that we would have recommended you anyway."

"Garrett Thomas?"

Repeat of the smile and chuckle.

"That's our man," Frank said.

My eyebrows raised. I appreciated compliments and affection, but I had no idea what had elicited that.

"You said Thomas and not Eggs."

I laughed. Evangeline Gonzalez Smith. Eggs. That was an obvious one that had not occurred.

"More than Eggs. I might have said Haskins if I wasn't mistaken."

"Not a lot of people know that," Bobby Z said.

"Not yet. And they won't hear it from me, but it's going to get out at some point."

"True," Frank agreed.

"What role do you two play?"

"We were introduced to Thomas, and we introduced Thomas to Haskins at some point. He has legislation coming out important to us that both are going to sign on board with. In return we helped him with Eggs."

I nodded. "A lot of the indigenous population might not be happy about that," I said.

"The legislation is important for the island and the

prior office holder didn't honor an agreement. Evy will get this done, and if she gets voted out next time, that's the way the ball bounces," Bobby Z said.

"The Big G is hard to read but he did seem to appreciate the fact we gave you the thumbs up, even though he had hired you. Apparently Evy really wanted you on board. A friend of hers suggested you to her and she wanted you," Frank told me.

"Have you met Todd?" I asked.

"Yeah, we warned Garrett about him," Bobby Z said.

"So did I," I replied.

"Garret could sometimes listen better," Frank said. "I wouldn't imagine you and Todd are getting along."

"He doesn't appreciate my sense of humor," I said, smiling.

"My money's on you, but that's 'cause we know you," Frank said. "He is not a push over."

"I know. I saw the videos."

"And let me guess," Bobby Z said. "You went out of your way to endear yourself to him."

"Let's just say that we aren't likely going to catch dinner and a movie sometime."

We all shook hands and I thanked them and said goodbye. Jeff and I went back to discussing the tail and the Cretella case. I needed to make the schedule less congested.

"Okay, so we know you are being followed, we have ascertained that is being done by Diane Cretella, and its grasping at straws. We can ignore it, or we can let them know we know and they will likely stop. But you said maybe we could use this somehow. Well, my son, how?"

"I'm thinking, Rabbi."

"I thought I smelled wood burning," Jeff said. "What do we know about Diane?"

"She is cruel and vindictive. She had hoped to coast and live on her ex's spousal and child support. Attractive, intelligent."

"Does she genuinely believe she's being attacked? I mean, does she actually think she's the good guy here?"

"The forensic shrink and her own doctor have her pegged as a textbook narcissist. She feels she's entitled to everything, and feels persecuted by the father fighting her for custody. Forensics also say she doesn't really want the kid, it's just the humiliation of not having the child and how that affects her image."

"Jesus, those poor kids," he said.

"Yeah."

"You know, it's my experience that most of the time the mother in these situations has been the better parent. I mean there are obvious exceptions, including this one," Jeff said.

"That's why everyone involved, if they are concerned about the welfare of the child, should look at each case on its own merits and leave any prejudice out of it," I replied.

"That's profound," he said.

"Thank you," I said, smiling.

"You didn't say that originally did you, son?"

"No, papa," I replied.

"Vachss?" he asked.

"Yup." We laughed.

"Well, Jeff, I learned from the best, pal. If it ain't you, it's him," I said.

"I'd argue if I could, son," he said.

We were quiet a while. I wondered for about the

millionth time what I could have done differently, and thought how whatever that was I would gladly do it, if I could see Mandy walk through the door and sit down and talk with me.

"So how can we use this to our client's advantage is the question," Jeff said.

"Well she does believe the husband, and me by association, are evil. Not because we hurt her kid or anything, but because we are standing in the way of what she wants." I shook my head. "Her lawyer called me a murderer in the judge's chambers. She would have no trouble believing anything bad about me."

"Hmmmmmmmmm. That should be useful. What if we showed her what she thought she would see?" Jeff asked me.

"While she had family members with political connections try to intervene in this case, she was accusing him of the same thing. She said he was a dealer, that he had large quantities of pain killers in his office, all of which are lies. Not just lies but proven to be lies."

"But she believed them?"

"Yes, and it was based on zero evidence. She basically thought it was true. She "knew" he was that kind of person."

"Wow," he said. He was quiet again for a bit but then he got that mischievous smile he would get when we were playing cards and he had pulled a bluff off. "I have an idea,"

I went outside and walked across the street to the sandwich shop and bought two sodas and saw that now both of my shadows were with me and I went in and got on the phone. I had made the calls and put everything in place for that evening. The key thing had been the cars and finding the right people that owned them. I had Tom drop what he was doing for me and work on it. I called my client and he wasn't happy about canceling plans that he had for that night but Jeff had called Rita his attorney and she loved the idea and she told him it was important for the case. It turns out Tom knew someone with the background I was looking for from church. What I was interested in were her priors. It took the rest of the day to set things up for that night. Fortunately, nothing popped on the blackmail case and we pulled it off.

8

I TOOK my time driving and went up the hill that lead to two of the colleges on the Island. St John's and Wagner. It had gotten a little colder and I knew exactly how the parking lot would be—a friend of mine taught a criminal justice class there at one of the colleges. The parking lot was full enough that my shadows could nestle in and hide but still have a good view of everything. I had put Tom and a couple of other people in place in different parts of the lot which was shared by both colleges. It sat on the top of a hill and behind it was a valley that lead to the harbor. The Verrazano Bridge was huge and lit up by lights and the enormous full moon that had risen behind it. The parking lot was very well lit to begin with but with the bridge and the moon it was almost daylight.

The key thing was to make sure that Peacoat and friend were able to get video, clear video. At the far end of the parking lot, the area furthest from the schools, there were two cars. My client stood outside of his car facing the vista. The other car was next to it with the plate clearly visible. The windows were dark and there was a driver but also someone crouched down next to the driver. I pulled parallel to them a good distance away. I had brought Cory with me but she stayed in the car. Although it had been warm, there was enough wind to make it uncomfortably cold but I got out of the car without a jacket. I had waited until I got the text from Tom that had said Campus PD had been spoken with, and with the right name drop they agreed to avoid the area. He was a car behind Peacoat and Danielle who had parked next to each other. He appeared to be having an animated conversation with his wife but he was actually watching them, and their eyes and phones were glued on us.

I walked toward my client with two clear plastic bags. One was filled with baking powder and the other with vitamin pills. The woman we had hired got out of the car. Tall, blonde, and beautiful, and a trooper. I say that because she was wearing just barely enough to qualify her outfit as clothing. Just barely. She stood there and the three of us spoke in low tones. Peacoat had no listening equipment.

"Hi, guys," I said, smiling. "Thanks for coming and thank you Kendra for helping us."

"Tommy is a good man. I owe him and I'm happy to help out."

I smiled and looked at Robert Perrone. "Take it and look it over good. Bob, let him see you do it do some bullshit thing like taste the baking powder. Take a couple of the pills. Don't worry, they're just zinc."

He nodded and we gestured as we spoke. Kendra shivered. I reached into my pocket and gave her some hundred dollar bills I had. Bob made a show of it and reached into his back pocket and took out an envelope that had cash in it. I made a show of counting it. When I looked at Kendra's car, I couldn't see Jeff slouched down in the back, even this close. My phone buzzed. It was a text from Tommy.

"This idiot must have another phone. He has Cretella on the line. I can hear him, his window is open." His wife, who used to join him often but not so much since the kids, sat next to him shooting video. Cory had video going since the office when I filled the bags with the baking powder and zinc tablets. Jeff had the video going in the back of the car. Bob's car was outfitted with multiple hidden cameras and had been since the half dozen false accusations Diane had made in an attempt to get an order of protection against him. It cost him a pretty penny and I made him spend a day with the guy that did the cameras learning to use it. There were two other people that worked for me in the parking lot. One shooting video of us, the other of Peacoat and Danielle.

"I'm freezing!" Kendra said.

"I'm sorry, kid," I said, smiling. "We are done now."

She smiled and put her arm around Bob and they went into the back of her car as I walked back towards my car careful to stay out of Cory's line of sight. Bob and Kendra got in the back of her car and then after about a minute, the three of them starting moving the car from the back so it looked like they were going at it in the back seat. I chuckled, imagining Jeff pushing himself back and forth with the two of them doing the same.

"They are high fiving each other and talking with Cretella on the phone. Everything they are saying is being recorded on the footage," read the next text from

Tom. I gave my phone to Cory, who had stopped filming, and asked her to text Tom for me.

"Okay, give them five and then have everyone break it off, let them leave. They should break off, too, and if so have everyone go back to the office. Make the master copy of the videos, the rest tomorrow. I notified Chief Marino and he will call the precinct commander and whoever is in narcotics tomorrow. They are certainly going to report this. I imagine I'll be served by 11 with an emergency order on for the afternoon. I'll need everyone on standby for testimony, although I doubt they actually will testify. See you in the morning."

"Done, boss," was the reply. I asked Cory to please dial Rita.

I spoke with her and filled her in and she was happy. She said that she'd already started the response to the legal papers she was likely going to be served with tomorrow morning.

We had a pool going as to how soon the Order To Show Cause would be served. I had tomorrow before noon for an emergency proceeding tomorrow afternoon. Rita had tomorrow afternoon with the proceeding the following morning, and Bob had us getting the papers the day after tomorrow.

Linda Smith Burns was Diane Cretella's attorney. She was her sixth lawyer. If you are in the know it's okay to change lawyers once even twice (if you just picked two bad lawyers) but more than that it was almost certainly that you were not hearing what it is you wanted to hear. Cretella was making Smith Burns rich. She had used her own considerable funds, borrowed from her mother, and did divorce funding. It was over half a million so far. Hell, it was fairly common knowledge to anyone except Cretella that Smith had hired a secretary for the primary purpose of dealing with her and working on her case. It was all smoke and mirrors. But it was working in some ways. In my client's case, had he done what Diane had, at best he would have supervised visits. All the forensics showed he was clearly the better parent. It was obvious Diane was abusive. It was obviously affecting the child.

In my experience, for the most part, and this is not stats and figures but observation, the mother was usually better suited for handling children, especially younger children, but that was not always the case. If a child was at stake it was incredibly important that the case be looked at prejudice free and on its own merits. I'd worked on cases in front of this judge where she had landed with both feet on the father for similar conduct yet she gave Diane chance after chance and delay after delay. It was costing my client thousands and costing the children their time as children. Rita had appealed and won so many decisions, and here we were at the end and the case was still ongoing, so that Diane could have me followed. For the sake of the kids, I hoped this ended it.

I had picked the morning because Burns had someone on staff burning through the checks that Diane wrote her. You'd need a mortgage or a home equity line of credit to pay for the bill Smith Burns would generate.

I won the pool.

Thursday morning it turned out there was a surprise. Truck and Danielle were legit. When I walked in the next morning Jeff was sitting at my desk smiling at me.

"Served?"

"Yes."

"Hah!" I said.

"And by the way, your tails work for Legal Stalkings LLC, and you are on YouTube."

"No!" I said, laughing. "Who the hell would name their firm Legal Stalkings?"

"You are going to be very happy," he said. He turned the laptop that was in front of him toward me and hit enter.

The screen went black and the fucking Pink Panther Theme came on. A little miniature Inspector Clouseau appeared on the screen with a magnifying glass.

"Oh dear God," I laughed.

"That was almost us," Jeff said.

"Over my dead body," I replied.

When we finally did a website the designer had suggested something similar to me. It took a few minutes of him smiling at me to realize that when I told him if he did that I'd kill him where he stood, I'd meant it. "People come to me when their lives or the lives of their children are at stake. I handle homicide investigations. I would not suffer that sort of embarrassment."

"Wait," Jeff said. "It gets better. Guess who owns Legal Stalkings?"

"Well come on, Jeff, give, who owns it?"

"Chester Green."

My jaw dropped. "No!"

Old Chester had worked for us a few years ago. He had been the referral of a friend and although he had been a cop, I never really looked into him prior to giving him work. He was adequate. That was the only time I had ever not done a background. After a few months it turned out nearly everything he ever told us was a lie and he was out there trying to take our clients. He had signed a non-compete clause that had been drawn up by Barren and Paris and that had been the cause of prolonged headaches and reactionary impotence for him. He would never get our clients. We were good and he had no clue, but it was embarrassing that he tried. Jeff had not been idle. He had been on the phone with the New York Department of State. Danielle and Bruno were properly printed and employed. Both were on w2s. And apparently there was video on the website and a description.

The phone rang. A few seconds later Mary called in from reception upstairs for me. I smiled as I always did when I heard her brogue.

"Umm, Jonathan, the *New York Wire* is on the phone."

"Jesus, I must have done something good in my life," I said to Jeff.

"Well you know you haven't, but hey, don't look a gift horse in the mouth, pal," Jeff said. Chester's wife also worked on staff at the *Wire*. I picked up the phone and said only my last name.

"Mr. Creed? I'm Jackie Helbock. I am a reporter for the *New York Wire*. We were given a tip and some video that we are doing a story on for Noon and I was wondering if you might want to give us a comment?"

"I will if I can, Ms. Helbock."

"Sir, did you participate in a drug deal at Wagner College last night?"

I grinned. With a little effort I made it sound as if I was troubled. "Ma'am, I can't comment on what I was doing last night because it's connected to an investiga-

tion we are handling. I can say, however, I do not participate in drug sales and I would take exception to that
allegation."

"So if we had video where it looked like you were
participating in a drug deal and we showed you," she
started.

"Miss Helbock, I can't comment but I can tell you I
don't deal drugs."

"Publicly when speaking at a Chamber of
Commerce meeting didn't you say that you felt the war
on drugs was a failure and the focus of the legal system
should be on crimes against children?"

"I did say that and I stand by it."

"Was your license ever investigated last year after
you killed Mark Stanton?"

"No, it wasn't, and it worked out that when Mr. Stanton, by shooting myself and my fiancée, caused me to
kill him in self-defense, I did the world a fucking favor.
You can quote me on that exactly."

"I can quote you on that?"

"You can, exactly. As a matter of fact, I wish it were
possible for me to kill him again."

I GOT on the phone and Jack Harmon picked up on the
second ring. I ran the whole scenario down for him.
He'd be at court.

Mike Mariano stopped by for coffee about a half
hour later and I gave him a copy of the report, the affidavits the office had prepared, and copies of the video. I
allowed him to examine the two bags Bob had dropped
off earlier with the Stevia and Zinc/Selenium pills. I also

gave him the dates and times I had been followed, prior. As a favor and to stop department resources from being wasted, he would stop off and see the precinct commander and the narcotics unit that happened to turn out of that precinct.

We were to be in court at two. Jeff put the TV on and Gotham News, the 24-hour news channel, had picked up the story from *The Wire*. I sent Al McLaughlin a message and he came downstairs a few minutes later. I told him what was going on and asked him how long it would take for him to send a letter out threatening defamation after I was done in court.

"It'll go out today," he said.

"Any objection to me sending letters to the grievance committee and the Bureau of Licensing Services about the attorney and the PI respectively?"

"None," he said.

A few hours later at court there was a full blown circus mid performance. News crews were outside, and there were reporters inside looking for space in the court room. The judge initially didn't want them as it was a matrimonial, but that only meant the file was confidential not the proceedings. This was far beyond what I had hoped for. The judge did have designs on higher office and that was common knowledge. Jack Harmon actually had a small office that the court officers gave him in the courthouse. He had a front row seat. He was not what the judge wanted to see.

Rita waited patiently as Smith Burns prattled on about drug deals and hookers. She ended with notifying the court that she had informed the police as it was her duty being an officer of the court and because of her grave concerns for the safety of the child. The law guardian and Rita patiently waited their turn. I was champing at the bit. The law guardian had also been furnished a copy of the answering papers, the affidavits, and copies of the videos.

About three rows back, Chester and his wife sat grinning. Rita got up slowly and spoke clearly, and by the time she was done, the judge had banged on her gavel at least four times. Chester and Diane Cretella sat there openmouthed. Smith Burns kept squeezing her eyes shut and her initial delight at all the free advertising had turned to a look like she had eaten something with mold on it. The judge asked for a meeting in chambers after the law guardian said she had reviewed the papers, and if the video supported it, that this was further evidence of the desperation of a mother that was unfit for her clients and she reaffirmed the wishes of the kids to live with their father. Harmon scribbled like a madman.

Apparently they watched a little of our videos on a laptop and the decisions were made. Smith Burns withdrew her order. At one point I was asked to go back to the judge's chambers. Off the record the judge told me that I had some balls manipulating the judicial system like that. I told her that being we were talking off the record that she had bigger balls contributing to the torture of two children because one of her goddamned cronies was pulling strings. I also told her that if she didn't make the final decision that I would give a full interview on television. I assured her any political future of hers would go right out the window. She screamed for her clerk and told him to get me the hell out of there. While all this was going on Mike Mariano had called the judge's chambers and asked to speak with me. No one had picked up the phone, and as I was being ushered out, the judge blew her last gasket and yelled, "Creed, there's a goddamned phone call for you!"

When I responded, "Would you mind taking a message, Judge?" the court clerk, whom I knew, who had the bad luck of the draw to end up with her, shoved me out of the room and I heard the judge's scream of anger cut off as the door closed.

"She can't hold you in contempt because it was off the record, Jimmy, but get the hell out of here," Christina Curry told me. I smiled, kissed her cheek, and left.

Outside the courthouse, Chester, Cretella, and Smith Burns were peppered with questions and followed back to their cars. I gave Harmon and Howard Thompson, who was a too little utilized investigative reporter for one of the local stations, an interview. I had carefully gone over everything I would say with Rita. My job was to help my clients, not to self-promote. I denied setting it up and gave an explanation for the video that, although plausible, everyone knew was bullshit.

Refusing to answer a question about the judge, Harmon did an aikido move on me, redirected me.

"Do you feel that too often judges take too long to decide these cases? This case has been going on for five years."

"Jack, I think children are children only for a short time. I think they shouldn't spend large chunks of their childhood with unfit parents when there are over-whelming facts to indicate a parent is unfit."

"So there's a limit, in your opinion, to parental rights?" Howard Thompson asked me.

"I think the rights of the child and the safety of the child should be the primary purpose of any court decision."

"Can you say if that is what is happening on this case?" Harmon asked.

"I can't, gentleman. I can't comment on an active custody case I'm working on."

We looked over when we heard screaming and saw across the street Diane Cretella verbally laying waste to her whole team. I heard Chester protesting, and she apparently had owed him some money because she tore a check into a million pieces and cursed him out in such a way that a Navy SEAL would blush. That was all caught on camera. I heard Chester tell her that he had hired Truck and Danielle because she wanted him to. Mystery solved there.

I left, and as I was walking toward my car I felt tired. Really tired. I hadn't slept much the night before. My phone vibrated as I got into my car a few blocks away.

9

THERE WAS nothing going on yet with the blackmail case. Eddie didn't have info yet and there were no new developments. I took Friday off, and Cory and I spent Friday into Saturday together. I recharged. We had rotating security and investigations going, although very little of the latter.

Mandy was with me, always. It hurt, always. I felt guilty when I was with Cory but she made me happy. The healing after the surgery had been slow and very painful. It didn't feel like I would ever be free from the pain of grief, but physically I was healing slowly but steadily. On Sunday I had dinner at one of my brothers. The family had gathered there. Cory was with her Dad and sister and she sent me a few text messages. A detective had come to see her about her ex. He had made bail and apparently he had a broken jaw as well as a missing tooth. There was an order of protection on him to stay away from her. Which of course meant there would be one issued for me as standard operating procedure. And that meant, because I had a carry permit, I had to forward that info to the NYPD licensing division. I hadn't been notified yet.

I got home Sunday night, and after taking care of the furry family, I sat and enjoyed a good book, *The Burning Season*, a PI novel written by Wayne Dundee. You had to be careful with the Hannibal novels. Dundee had this habit of making it seem like everything was okay, mission accomplished, and then he killed a character you had come to care about. Bastard.

I got a text from Cory inquiring if I might be interested in what was commonly called a booty call. I responded Hell Yes! And the doorbell rang less than a minute later. She was there with a huge grin on her face and told me she'd had been sitting in her car when she sent the message.

The rest of the night, the end of the weekend, had been a lot more fun than I had thought it would be, all deference to Wayne Dundee aside. On Monday things would start to break on the blackmail case, and in the coming weeks I would look back very fondly on the past three days.

10

I GOT in fairly early on Monday. Cory had been over till very late I missed some sleep but I was not unhappy about why. I finally looked at the videos that Tony had sent me. There were three MMA fights that Todd had won by knockout. Once with a punch and once with a goddamned spinning back kick. The guy was just about out anyway and Todd was showing off. The last was when he took this guy down and did a ground and pound and shoved the ref off him when the ref tried to break it up. He was disqualified for that. The other fighter was now out of the fight game and most people said it was because of the injuries he got from Todd. There were videos of him training as well. He had a penchant for knocking out sparring partners. He was cruel and vicious. He was also damned good. He ran about two sixty and he didn't carry any fat. In one video he did a ground and pound on a sparring partner and he told whoever was holding the camera that's what people who disrespected him got. Charming. I had simultaneously a hope that I'd get to see how good he was and a hope that I didn't.

Eddie met me as I walked in and asked me to talk with him in the office once I was ready.

"That email was sent from their Wi-Fi."

My eyebrows raised. "Okay, how? I mean was it hacked from another location?"

"Probably someone sitting in a car, with a laptop."

"Can you contact them, or get them to contact me?"

"I can try but I'd have someone," he started.

"Sitting outside, watching the block." I finished for him.

He smiled. "There's no telling when the next email will come."

I was at the campaign headquarters twenty-five minutes later. I talked with Tony and told him what was going on. He said he would fill in Jimmy Hannan and the other guys. I told him we didn't really have anything yet not to let on about it.

"Do me a favor and ask Jimmy Hannan if he wouldn't mind coming early and sitting outside, see if a car ends up sitting there, and if so, get me a plate."

He called Jimmy and I listened. He was bored and didn't mind the money. He got there before I left. He had a slight tint on his windows and parked and got into the back seat without us noticing him do so. We didn't acknowledge him.

Another email would come the next afternoon. It was one of the first actual winter days we had. It was dreary and cold. The wind bit into you and made you happy to be inside. The girls in the office hadn't taken down the Christmas decorations yet; we waited until little Christmas, as I did at home. I didn't intend on decoration this year but you never knew when one of the nieces or nephews might have stopped by. The girls at the office would replace the Christmas decorations with Valentine's Day stuff. I had a good crew.

On Tuesday Tony had texted me everything was in place. Cory had called and we talked a bit and she brought a smile to my face. She was going to be at the campaign later. I told her I'd see her there. Jeff and I walked out the back to our cars at the same time. I got to mine first and said goodbye and was pulling up to the campaign when he called.

"Miss me already, Papa?" I asked him.

"Not in the least, son, pain in the ass. But you need to know you have another tail."

"What?"

"Black Toyota Camry. New. Pulled out when you did. Shot to the stop sign and turned left to follow you. It's a tail or I'm senile."

"Maybe both, pal," I said as I watched the Camry pass me. It went too fast for me to get the plate and there were two other cars behind it. "Just passed me. I couldn't grab the plate. Damn, I wasn't looking for it."

"You ain't that interesting," he said.

"Tell me about it. What the fuck, Jeff? Cretella? Again?"

"I don't know, son, but be careful."

As I sat outside Tony texted me. I had stopped at a place near the office called "Cup O Joe," where, despite the missing letter, they made great coffee.

"Hey, Boss, activity. Another email."

The drive over had been less than ten minutes. As I was getting out, Todd was leaving in a hurry. I watched him jog to a red Jeep Cherokee. He left a little rubber. Probably late for a NAMBLA meeting.

I got in and Tony was waiting. We went off to the small alcove that he had made the security office and spoke low enough to keep the conversation private.

"Before I knew, Evy told Todd. She told me, I sent you the text, and Todd and Garrett were in Garrett's office. I asked him what was up but he brushed me off."

I shook my head. "I start every case off trying to tell the client what the best moves are. When they don't listen I get it in writing, and I make the money until they fire me because they decided not to listen and they are pissed it didn't work out."

"So what's the problem, Jimmy? Me and Hannan don't mind standing post for this pay. You're making a killing. Do what you normally do."

"I got a feeling here, Tony. Something is wrong. Listen, you guys are both out of rotation tonight and tomorrow, right?"

"Yeah, first days off since it started."

"I may need back up since my tail is back."

"Seriously? Why? They just lost the case."

"I don't know for sure it's them, but they are all I can think of. I got a profile on that knucklehead that was following me. He's at Karaoke every Tuesday night. I'm not familiar with the bar and might need someone watching my back."

"Tomorrow night? We will be there. What time?"

"Nine."

"I hate when you get feelings," he said.

"Well, that bad feeling is about this damned case. Where the hell did Todd go I wonder?"

"Have you considered that they are politicians and

therefore almost certainly liars, narcissists, and sociopaths, and that's what you don't like?"

"Why hire me to help them with blackmail, if they don't want me to help? They know more." He shook his head and shrugged. "Ah well off to see the Wizard," I said.

"Pay no attention to that man behind the curtain," he said as I moved off.

"That's why I have you. When you see him, shoot."

Garrett was waiting for me. Evy sat across from him and they each had coffee. I said hello and took up the empty chair.

"What have we got?"

He reached over and handed me a printed email. "I have my cyber people working on it."

I shook my head. "Garrett, I have people on it. Tony told you that. That's making it congested. You have to have faith and give us a chance to do our job."

"You're right, it's just frustrating," he said.

I nodded and read it. "You need to pay what you should. You know why. If you don't, I'll tell the world about you and that whore you own. If she doesn't drop out, maybe you'll both read about it in the news."

"Why the hell don't they say what they have on you?"

"To my knowledge I haven't done anything wrong."

I sighed. "Evy, any input?"

"Hmmmmm? Uh, no. I don't know what she means. It has to be the far right."

"It doesn't look that way to me. It seems personal."

"Climate deniers and capitalists take it very personal because I'm a threat to them."

I nodded. "I get that, but do me a favor would you?

When you don't know for sure and you make an assumption, you tend then to overlook things that could help. It's like when the cops arrest the wrong guy."

"They arrest the wrong guy all the time," she said.

"Evy, forget politics and views. I do criminal defense work and I have for twenty-five years. Most of the time the cops are right. Well over ninety percent of the time. When they are wrong, it is because someone got tunnel vision, assumed that it was what it usually is, and looked no further. Can we please look at it that way until this is over? My job is to find this person and keep you safe, and I need you working with me on that not against me."

The look on her face, which was that I was a species of parasitic fungus and she had me under a microscope trying to figure out how to rid the world of me, indicated I was in store for a lecture. And there was animus. I realized that it was likely because of Cory. As I took a deep breath and prepared to deal with it and find another way to make my point, Garrett broke in.

"He is right, Evy. We asked him to help us, and he needs our help to do so."

Although I was relieved it was only to a point. Garrett was very good at manipulation. He was placating both Evy and I. He didn't need to know that I knew that, though. I often found it to be to my advantage when people thought I was stupid or that they were smarter than me. I nodded for effect and was gratified Garrett read it like I wanted him to.

"More so than that, Garrett, you are paying me and paying me well. I know money isn't an issue but it's not good for anyone to just throw it away. And although it may be that this person or persons are non-violent, we can't know they aren't. You have people, a lot of people, volunteers who believe in you guys that are giving their time. We don't want them as collateral damage."

He nodded.

"So what can I do?" Evy asked, clearly to please Garrett.

"Keep an open mind and think about it from every angle you can," I said.

It was no surprise to me that people would hire me, pay me a lot of money to help them, and then sabotage themselves. Often they created the problem and then wanted to hire me and micro manage me. So essentially it was "you created this situation, you're in grave danger because of it, and now using the same methodology, you want to run how I fix it for you?"

When that happened it was simple. It was my obligation to explain to the client why they were making a mistake. If they listened, great. If they didn't, I'd cover my tracks with an email or something in writing and then I would take the money anyway.

Todd strolled in, got a quick embrace from Garrett, a smile from Evy, and a nod from me. He didn't bother to return it. He went off to his office and closed the door. I told them I would be back and if they needed me or heard anything to call me immediately.

I stopped off to see Tony. He had a coffee waiting for me. I sat on the edge of the small desk and took a sip. He was finishing a call to his wife. He hung up and looked at me.

"Todd has an office now."

"So I saw. He is a man moving up in the world."

Tony snickered. "Did you see those videos I sent you?"

"I did."

"And?"

"He's very good. He is also vicious and cruel. He had no business hurting those sparring partners, he only did so for the camera. And he kept hitting that guy even when the ref tried to pull him off."

"Thus the suspension."

"Yeah."

We both paused to download some java. Coffee did make everything better.

"It does make everything better," I said aloud.

"Coffee?"

"Yeah."

"Todd doesn't drink it."

"Why am I not surprised," I said with a snort. "The only thing that would make Todd better would be a simultaneous castration and lobotomy."

"He doesn't think much of you, boss. He hasn't been kind."

"I am wounded," I said.

"I doubt that, but he is not a kind person," he emphasized. "I asked and then warned him not broach certain subjects with you."

My eyebrows raised. "Such as," I asked.

"Jimmy, I'd rather not discuss it. I think I talked some sense into him and I'd rather leave it alone."

I considered that. If it went in the direction I thought it would, it would result in my kicking in Todd's door and driving his teeth out the back of his head. With everything going on that would not be a good strategy.

"Let me guess," I said. "Stanton."

"Along those lines."

I shook my head. "You are right, Tony. Although

knocking him around would be fun, but hardly productive here." I paused. "Not to mention, it might not be all that easy to do."

"I'd pack a lunch, Jimmy."

"Yeah."

Todd came strolling through the front door in all his glory. He immediately walked up to us and stood there, arms folded.

"Hey, Todd," Tony said.

Todd nodded at him dismissively. That pissed me off. Tony didn't deserve that from this shit head.

"Got anything for us, Creed?" he asked me.

"Yes, Todd, advice. You may know how to use your hands but you don't know shit about protection, investigations, or respect for that matter. I also do not work for you. If I have anything to report it will be to Garrett, and if you start acting like a professional, I may include you in the info. Now move along."

I didn't mince words with him. The response was exactly what you'd think it would be. His face got red and his anger was evident.

"Now I kept my voice low, Todd, intentionally, so I did not embarrass you. I will treat you as your conduct merits. Being we are working for the same people and have the same goal in mind or should have, why don't we start over. Let's both take a deep breath and try talking to each other like professionals with courtesy and respect."

"Fuck you," he said. His tone, unlike mine carried. The room went quiet. Cory had apparently come in while I was with Garrett and Evy. Evy had come out while we were talking and had moved over to where Cory was. I smiled at Cory and she smiled back and blew me a kiss. She was worried and we were talking in the corner and they watched along with everyone else.

"No thanks, Toddster, you're cute but not my type."

"Fuck..." he started to say and caught himself. I grinned. "We don't need you," he said.

"Somehow, Toddy, I don't think we are going to be besties," I said.

"Don't make fun of my fucking name, old man."

"Oh Toddenheimer, you're cute when riled up but still, not my type."

The room remained quiet. We were only a few feet apart. I could feel his energy, coiled up and looking for release like a grenade just before the pin was pulled. No, that was wrong. It was like old sweating dynamite, being loaded onto a truck. You have no idea when and if it would go off, but if it did, there would be body parts all around.

"I could wipe the floor with you," he said.

"Well, Toddster, there ain't no wall between you and me."

"I told you," he said advancing a step, "don't make fun of my name."

"Well the thing is, one, it's a great name to make fun of, and two I really enjoy it." I stepped closer to him.

As he opened his mouth to say something Garrett walked in. He saw what was going on and moved toward us.

"Gentlemen, please, let's go into my office and talk a bit."

Before Garrett could talk, I did. Todd was standing there boring holes into me with his eyes. He puffed his chest out and his face was red.

"Listen to me, you tomato can. Being good with your

hands doesn't make you an expert in security and investigations. You do as I say or I walk. End of story." I looked at Garrett. "You hired me to help you, and this jackass running about throwing his weight around isn't helping. It's ridiculous to have people working on the same thing and not cooperating."

Garret was silent for a minute.

"Are you and I clear, Garrett? I'm not going to have this guy working against me because he has something to prove. If that's the case, I'll pull out, generate a report and bill, refund what's due, if anything, and I'm done. That is in my retainer. It's hard enough tracking down a fucking ghost. I don't want strong arm tactics being used where I could end up with a complaint on my license."

Garrett nodded. "Todd, we did agree that Jonathan would run the show. Please, I know it comes from a good place and you want to help, but we agreed to listen to him."

"Fine, Garrett." He stormed off to his office.

Tony came back in and he Garrett and I discussed some of the events we had coming up, and I noticed the Toddster coming back, a bit irritated it appeared.

"Listen, let me tell you something," he seethed. "I got a record of seven and two. I got six wins by knockout. I could wipe up the floor with you, so watch what you call me."

I realized what happened, and despite my best efforts I burst out laughing. I actually laughed so hard I just about doubled over. Tony was grinning, Garrett had no idea what was going on, and Todd stood there face red and anger oozing out his pores.

"For God's sake, Todd," Garrett said. "What's wrong?"

"He looked up tomato can on the internet," I said.

My phone vibrated that it required attention, and I looked at the number. The office. Still laughing, I asked them to excuse me and walked out the front of the headquarters. Mary's soft brogue greeted me and mentioned that Eddie Martin was asking when I was getting back, that he needed to see me.

Eddie rarely used phones, even burner phones. He had his office swept regularly. I made more money from him doing that than I did from his paying rent. I had a guy who was a top notch pro, Dennis, in Long Island. He was in our office once a month for Eddie and once in a while I'd have the whole building done. Bottom line was if you wanted to see him, you went to his office. Which was my office.

I grabbed Cory and we went into Tony's room for a bit and talked.

"Wow, what was that about?"

"Todd is a mite challenged and isn't aware of courtesy that should be afforded to other human beings."

"Oh, you mean he acted like an asshole. Again."

"Yeah."

"Be careful with him, okay?" Her eyes searched mine and she was serious. "I know you can take care of yourself but he is a very cruel person. He hurt some poor man and Garrett paid a lot of money to get him out of it. He wanted to fix me up with him and I refused."

I smiled. "That's probably one reason the Toddster and I don't like each other," I said. I asked her if she wanted to have dinner tonight and she couldn't but asked if we could tomorrow.

"I have business first, sweetheart, but it won't be all night."

"Then I'll be dessert."

"I love it when you're dessert," I said.

She kissed me and I held her a while and stroked her hair. I could feel she was a little tense.

"I promise I'll be okay," I told her.

"Okay." She smiled at me and kissed me again.

I got back and saw Eddie and he told me that he'd have something for me in another day or so, he hoped. By something he meant a way for me to contact them.

Tuesday was paperwork, checking several times for a tail, and asking Eddie Martin if he had anything. I used the day to catch up on paperwork and think about my clients. They could provide no clue as to who might be blackmailing them. They seemed reluctant to help. Todd was being sent on secret missions. I was making a ton of money on it. Why the hell had they hired me? As the Camry never reappeared, Tuesday night was on.

We all went about our business until nine-thirty. Jimmy, Tony, and I met at the Great Kills Tavern. There was a sign up announcing music and karaoke by Loren. I smiled. Loren Utt was a Country Western singer. He did a show that included karaoke and sometimes dancing. There was a drop dead gorgeous woman in a cowboy hat, Daisy Duke shorts, and looking like something a cowboy would see if he died and went to heaven. She had this cute button Irish nose and these huge brown doe eyes. When she smiled it was like a spotlight. If you were a heterosexual male or a gay woman, best to surrender up front.

I watched as she turned and walked toward the back. Good legs, too. Tony spoke and brought me back to reality.

"There's your boy." He jerked his head toward a

second room and sure enough, there was Truck. He was there with four other guys and some girls. On closer inspection one was Danielle. But he was with another girl if the seating arrangements were any indication.

"How do you want to play this?" Jimmy Hannan asked. To save on confusion since we were younger and he was a little older, when we were all together I was referred to as Jonathan and he was Jimmy, although there were frequent slips. Alcohol added inevitably to the confusion. "Want me to go over there and smack him a few times?"

I snorted. "That would be fun," I admitted. "But let's go a little more civil. No point in trying to disguise why we are here," I said and signaled the waitress. The waitress came over and I judged her to be a woman of good taste as her eyes were also fixed on the cowgirl. I pointed out Peacoat's table and asked her to give them a round on me. I gave her a hundred dollar bill and told her to keep the change.

I was sitting in such a way that they couldn't see my face clearly. Tony saw her bring the drinks and the waitress pointed in our direction. Tony waved in response. He made a quick suggestion and we agreed. He got up to use the men's room and passed by the table and said hi. I knew them and it was a gesture to Danielle and Truck. Tony went in the bathroom and Truck and Danielle, after looking at each other quizzically, came over.

Shock registered on their faces when I turned and raised my glass to them. Jimmy was quiet, his eyes on Truck. I still preferred Peacoat.

"Long time no see," I said, smiling. "I figured what's

the chance of us bumping into each other and as we are in the same business, let me say hi. So, hi."

They both looked at me and each other. "I'm sure Chester didn't instruct you as to what to do in a situation like this, but—"

"He fired us, jerkoff," Bruno snarled at me. I smiled wider. Hannan would get his chance.

"Now that is no way to talk, Truck. Do you prefer Truck? Or Bruno? I have come to call you Peacoat, in my head, because you cut such a dashing figure in one. While you failed at being inconspicuous, you certainly made quite the fashion statement," I informed him. His face got very red. Danielle stood there not knowing what to do. Truck was trying to figure out how to act while I was making fun of him.

He leaned forward, both hands on the table, and snarled at me, while using a stare that he must have practiced in the mirror every day. I shook my head. Jimmy moved. He drove his thumb into Peacoat's neck, to the side of his windpipe.

"Gak," said Bruno, hands going to his throat. It happened fast and no one noticed. Jimmy got up and asked him "Hey, pal, are you okay?" He then double hooked him in the gut, twice with the same hand, faster than you could see. It bent him over and Jimmy helped him onto the chair.

Danielle froze. "Sweetheart, no one's going to hurt you. You can go if you want. No one was going to hurt him until he made his move first. But if you can, I'd like to just ask a couple of questions."

She sat also and looked at us. Tony got back after he had stopped off and spoke to the others at Peacoat's table. It was crowded the music had started. Peacoat tried to breathe. I watched the cowgirl and wondered where the hell would I apply for the job of painting those jeans on.

"Are you guys still on this case? Is Chester still having me followed?"

She shook her head. "He fired us. He didn't even give us the money he owed us."

"How much?" I asked her.

"Two hundred each."

I reached into my pocket and took out six one hundred dollar bills. I put three in front of her and three in front of Bruno. Bruno, although gasping, took notice. He looked at me.

"Yes, Truck," I said as I nodded to him. "I just want fifteen minutes and some questions answered."

They looked at each other and she nodded to him. "He put us on this, paid us next to nothing, and he knew we never did this before. Now he won't pay us. What do we owe him?"

She was the smart one apparently. Chester never was one to do the right thing. But that was partly my fault. He broke bread with my family on holidays and I gave him a good amount of work and he tried to steal my clients. I was hoping for something like this. Truck nodded.

"Ever do this kind of work before?"

They both shook their heads. "Tell me how you got it and what happened, what you were told."

"I know Diane. She was my neighbor and she hired my real estate firm because I got her a discount. We were together a few times. She asked me to help her. She was given the PI by her lawyer. She was paying them a lot of money, and I thought I'd go the extra mile for her. She and I had a thing. She had asked me if I might be able to do anything to help her. I didn't know what she meant in the beginning."

"What did you come to learn she meant?" Jimmy asked him.

He kept his head down; hard to look a man in the eye that just smacked you around.

"She wanted me to like plant drugs or something. I told her I couldn't do that. I'm a realtor, I got a license and two kids I gotta pay support for."

"And you?" I asked the girl.

"We went to school together. We are friends, and I needed the work."

"Neither of you ever did a tail job before?"

They both shook their heads.

"Did he teach you anything?"

They shook their heads again. "He told us what to do and said to call if we had any questions. He didn't have anyone to work on the holidays."

"Why exactly did she want me followed?"

"She said you conspired with her husband to steal her kids. She said you were a murderer and a drug dealer."

Tony snorted and he and Jimmy exchanged glances. I watched the two of them. "I assume you know that was a lie?"

They nodded.

"Do you know if he has someone else following me?"

"He and his wife went away on vacation. She was fired from her job because of what happened, after your lawyer called the paper where she worked. He said this was our fault."

"It's not your fault. You had no experience and no one trained you to do the job," I said.

"She paid him a lot of money. I saw a check on his desk from her for fifty thousand dollars. She really thought he would do something like plant drugs on you."

"He couldn't find his ass with both hands and a flashlight. The reason he didn't show you how to do the tail job is he isn't good at that himself."

"I'm sure he doesn't have anyone following you. He called us from Colorado. He went skiing. He didn't know anyone else. It's why he used us."

"Okay," I told them. "Thank you. It was a rough start but it wasn't your fault." Truck kept his head down but the girl looked at me. Truck mumbled something to me and took his money and left. The girl stayed and looked at us.

"I always wanted to do PI work." She did seem like a nice kid.

My phone vibrated; it was Cory. She sent me a picture of herself in silk shorts and some kind of top that was not meant to be worn outside of the boudoir. It read "I can be over in twenty minutes."

"I have something that absolutely must be attended to," I said. I left two hundred more on the table. "I'm sure the guys will be happy to talk with you about it, and in a week or so come and see me and I'll see if I can give you some direction."

Tony looked at me. "The lovely bride hasn't seen me in a bit, so I'm going to light out, too."

Jimmy looked at Danielle. "I have nowhere to be, pretty lady, if you don't."

She smiled at him and sat closer to him and they

started talking. I went to the car. We had intentionally all parked near each other, and Tony and I said our goodbyes and went off to our own separate adventures.

I'm pretty sure I blew past at least three red light cameras and achieved warp factor nine on the way home. Worth it.

11

I GOT out of the shower and Cory was still sleeping. She didn't have to be anywhere today and I was quiet so she could sleep. I was downstairs having my second cup of coffee and thinking about a cigar when I got a message on my phone from the office. Eddie was asking for me.

Ten minutes (one of the great things about working in the City's smallest borough) later, I sat with Eddie and had more coffee in an attempt to set the world's record for having the highest blood pressure. I had been eager to see Eddie, but when I got to the office I sat in the parking lot for a while. The Camry passed me; he or she was good but this time I had gotten the plate number. There was possible a second car I hadn't made yet. I thought about Mandy and Vicki. I missed Cory and then felt guilty. My heart raced but not from the abundance of caffeine. That feeling of panicked loss was trying to work its way in. I closed my eyes and for what would have been the millionth time said to the universe I'd give anything it wanted to get her back. I paused in my office to run the plate. It came back to a car rental company.

Grief and pain like this, you never got over it. Ever. It was a matter of learning to tolerate it. I wasn't having much success there. No matter how I tried to reason it out, she was dead and it was my fault. Her son would grow up without his mom. I'd never hold her again. See her again except in memory. And Vicki fighting to save her kids and dying alone and afraid.

If someone else told me this story, I'd have told them it wasn't their fault. So why was it mine? Why? Because it is.

A deep breath and ten minutes later I sat with Eddie. We had coffee and spoke a little before getting down to business. Not for the first time I looked at the cherubic information broker and knew that no one would guess what he did.

"I got a number," he said as he slid a piece of paper across the table to me.

"And this is whose number?"

"Ninety percent certain this is your blackmailer."

"Okay, Eddie, I don't want you to tell me exactly or give your secrets away but how the hell," I asked.

He laughed. "I took it a step farther than Garrett's people. I found a burner phone number that had been purchased and internet service ascribed to it. Paid in advance a year. Whoever did it made the mistake of not doing it from far enough away."

"Okay, I get the idea," I said, knowing that was far beyond what most PIs or even government agencies would have access to. I thought about the time Mary had told me that the Whitehouse Chief of Staff called him.

"You're a good man, Jonathan," he told me. "You help people, you are one of the good guys. I don't mind working with you at all."

"I certainly wouldn't ordinarily be able to afford you as often as I use you, Eddie. I do appreciate it."

"It's my pleasure." We sat there a minute. "How are you feeling? You must be tired of that question, but most of us are worried about you."

"I'm okay, Eddie. I'm as good as I could be."

He nodded.

"How are you with getting information from car rental companies?"

"Like taking candy from a baby."

I gave him the plate number and the name and address of the rental company. I wondered, honestly, what he couldn't find out.

I looked at the number on the piece of paper that he gave me. A 718 area code and followed by five 5's and two 9's. It had to go back to an app or something like that. I took out my phone and sat behind my desk. I decided texting was the way to go. I thought about it for a while and decided I'd send a text but I'd wait a while before I did.

An hour later I got a text from Tony. We got an email, and just after we did a beat up old Corolla with a personalized license plate pulled out."

I texted him back. "Hold onto that number, do not give it to me yet."

"Affirmative."

I sent the text. "I believe you are the person emailing my clients G and E. I believe I can act as a middle person and help you get what you want. If you agree to talk or meet I give you my word, I won't try to find out who you are."

I was getting hungry. It rarely seemed there was a time when I wasn't. I was always an all or nothing guy. If I worked out in the morning, I would eat well and drink moderately and the sweet tooth would be held at bay.

"You left a message for me," came from a number that consisted of only nines.

"Can we please meet? You have my word no attempt will be made to inhibit you or follow you."

"You work for Garrett Thompson?"

"I work for myself. I was hired by his lawyer. I set the terms. I can give you references if you want to check me out. He won't know about it until after we meet. I won't try to find out who you are or follow you," I texted back. "You have my word," I added.

"The Colonnade Diner at nine p.m." came ten minutes later.

"Good," my response said.

I looked at my watch. I hated napping during the day not just because it made me feel old but because it would throw my sleep cycle off. I was a little hungry. I called Cory and it went to her voice mail. I drove back to the office and thought about Mandy and Vicky. I had managed to get two women I cared about killed. I wonder if that is some kind of record?

I called Bobby Bianchi and he was free. We decided to have lunch at Italianissimo. Despite my dark thoughts, my stomach rumbled and I smiled. Franco the owner was a good friend. The food was absolutely superb. By the time I got to the restaurant, there was a bottle of great red wine on the table. Bobby had ordered a couple of appetizers and they were arriving. He kissed my cheek when I got to the table.

"Jimmy Hannan had called me he said he was working for you on that political thing. He had some time to kill and Tito Alvarez was with him and I asked them to join us."

I smiled, a genuine smile. Jimmy and Tito, like so many of the people I grew up with, were important to me. Shortly the three of us got lost in memories of childhood and it ended up being a great afternoon. I stayed there until eight, leaving only because I had a date with a mystery at the Colonnade at nine.

There were only a few cars in the parking lot. There was an older Corolla, blue or black, that was parked on the street on the west end of the parking lot. It's license plate read "Beezy."

I walked in to find Marco the owner there. He was almost ninety, but he looked sixty and had a wit faster than most. I had met him back in 1989 when I handled a personal injury case someone had brought against the diner. It was one of the first trial preps I did for Jim O'Donnell. Marco handled himself on the witness stand like a pro. I asked him for a table in the back so I could have a little privacy. I didn't look around outside. I had my phone out and was reading from the Kindle app. In case he, she, or they were watching.

"I'm here, last booth in the back on the left hand side."

A girl whom I had passed that was alone and drinking coffee in a booth looked at me. She looked at her phone and then put it away. I bet she had someone watching the outside and they gave her the thumbs up. She drank some more coffee and then got up took her cup and came over to my booth. She sat down and looked at me. She was young, maybe twenty. I had a complex set of rules. Cory, who was close to thirty, was about as young as I would go with romantic interest. As I got older that age increased. Appraising her in an objective way netted that she was tired. She was also nervous but hid it well. Her hair was long, well past her shoulders but the sides were much shorter and the length of her hair sometimes gave the illusion when she moved that all her hair was that long. She was pretty despite the nose ring. I always wondered if a good sneeze might actually blind a friend.

Her body language, for what that subjective and unreliable pseudo-scientific method suggested, was that she was determined. About what I had no idea yet. She was appraising me as well. Neither of us broke the silence. There was something else about her. After over 20 years of my work I was rarely wrong. She was in trouble. Not that there was a profile for it but looking at her, blackmail was not anywhere near the first thought I would have.

I held my hand out, across the table. She looked at it and then me and then at my hand again. She started to reach for my hand, stopped and then grasped my hand firmly.

"I'm Jonathan. I also go by Jimmy sometimes."

"Rain."

"That is a beautiful name."

She didn't say anything. But I garnered a little more about her as time went by. She was not tired, she was exhausted.

"Would you like me to start or would you prefer to?"

I asked her. As she didn't answer, after thirty seconds or so I spoke.

"I would like to find out what your purpose is in blackmailing my client."

Her eyes widened a little and she gave a short sarcastic laugh. "Blackmail? Are you fucking kidding me?"

"What would you call it?"

"Trying to get what is due me and my—" She stopped at that and looked out the window.

"And your...?" I asked.

She shook her head. "He owes me that money."

"Why?"

"He knows why. You work for him. You should know."

"I don't. He tells me he has no idea who is sending him these notes."

The sarcastic laugh again.

"What are you exactly?"

"Do you mean besides devilishly handsome, charming, and modest?" I grinned as I asked it. She came close to smiling but didn't. "In this instance I'm a licensed private investigator," I said, taking out my State issued id card and showing it to her.

She looked at it carefully. She nodded to herself. I also handed her a business card with the cell number she already had on it and as well as email company website, etc. She took it and looked at me.

"He hired you to deal with me?"

"Well, first to find you."

"And he told you what?"

"That he was being blackmailed and that he wanted me to find out who was doing it and what they wanted.

It appeared that he was amenable to a solution and making this stop."

"If he was I wouldn't be here," she said.

"I read the note, at least one of them, Rain. It said *I won't go away until you honor your debt.*"

"I sent that to him," she confirmed.

"And you don't feel that is blackmail?"

"He has a debt, an obligation."

"I notice you don't say he doesn't have a debt to you," I said.

"That's right. It's not to me."

"Then to who?" I asked.

"He knows. He goddamned well knows."

"Why not tell me?"

She shook her head.

"Are you hungry?"

She hesitated and shook her head. Another thing I knew about people was when they were hungry. Food was the oldest and most successful relationship I'd had. I raised my hand and the waitress acknowledged me from across the room.

"I've eaten but they have the best cheesecake in the city here, after mine. Please order something."

She shook her head.

"Listen, it's rude to make me eat alone, and besides that, kid," she looked up at me, "Garrett is paying for it."

She ordered a burger and fries and told me she was ordering something to go but she'd pay for that. I nodded. She asked the waitress for chicken nuggets and fries. She ordered a coke, too. I got cheesecake and regrettably, decaf.

"Okay, if you can't tell me why he owes someone and

who that someone is, tell me about you and why you're the debt collector."

"Nothing to tell. I'm a typical Z. You think I'm stupid and I think you're old."

"But devilishly handsome, don't forget," I said. She almost smiled again. "And, I might not be smart but I can lift heavy things."

She did smile that time.

"I will tell you what, Rain, let us make an agreement, just you and I. We are not obligated to tell each other everything, but let us agree to be honest in what we tell each other. That is a start."

"But you work for him."

"No. I work for myself. That is an important distinction. And in this instance, I work for his lawyer."

"He has a lot of those."

I sensed there was a personal knowledge here, although it was common knowledge and not any great feat of deductive reasoning that the G man employed more attorneys than some *Fortune 500* companies. We sat a bit longer and the food arrived. By the time she had put ketchup on the plate for the fries and cut the hamburger in half I had finished half my cheesecake. As I got up to use the bathroom, she watched me stand. I took my phone out and my keys and put them on the table so she saw I wasn't going to make a call. She nodded to herself. I went to the bathroom and saw the waitress, Maddie, whom I knew from being there. She was tall and slim and her hair was long, blonde, and curly, almost ringlets. I put a hundred dollar bill in her hand.

"That's for the whole check, Maddie, her to go order

also. Please take twenty out for yourself and give me a receipt when we are done."

Maddie was smart. She knew me and that sometimes I met people there because of work. If I was alone or if she got a negative answer in reply to "are you working?" she'd chat. Otherwise, she'd be scarce.

"You got it, hun," she told me, smiling. "I'm waiting for you guys to get further along before I put the "to go" order in so it stays warm when she gets home to her kid."

"How do you know it's not lunch for tomorrow?" I asked her.

"I've seen her around. She's got a kid. They were in here twice and all the baby eats is chicken nuggets," she told me. "I see her at the Stop & Shop every once in a while, too. She always has the baby."

"Keep the change and just give me the receipt," I said.

"Thanks!" she said.

"Oh," I turned back toward her. "How old is the baby?"

"Four or five I think," she said.

I took a chance. "She drives that old Toyota Corolla right, the beat up one with the personalized license plate?"

"Yeah, it's her neighbors. He's an older man and she helps him with shopping and stuff since he can't drive anymore."

"Thanks."

———

WHEN I GOT BACK she'd eaten half of the burger and some of the fries. She eyed me as I sat. I finished the cheesecake in about four more seconds. It really was good. I preferred mine because I used a chocolate graham cracker crust but it was great. I placed it a half step above Junior's in Brooklyn. But, that may have been influenced by proximity.

She was quiet as she ate. I thought about Cory for a bit which as usual brought Mandy and then Vicki in to the present. Although the negotiations phase of grief should have passed long ago I said mentally to whoever was listening that I'd give anything for Mandy to be back.

"Okay," I said. "You can't tell me why Garrett has the debt with you, so what can you tell me?"

"What do you want to know?"

"What are your intentions, to start. What is it you will do if he doesn't satisfy that debt?"

"I don't know."

"Okay, let's start with what you won't do."

She looked at me.

"Would you hurt him? Physically I mean. Or Evy?"

"Even if I wanted to, how could I?"

"People are easy to hurt, and if you can't you can always find someone that could."

"Like you?" she asked me.

"I don't do that kind of thing. I protect people, I gather information. I'm not a strong arm, kid. You don't have to worry about that with me. But," I continued and now I had her attention. "I'm not the only one working for him, and I have no idea how genuinely threatened he feels by you."

"It's not that he wouldn't deserve it, but I have

responsibilities. And you could be lying to me, trying to gain my confidence. Anybody can hurt people and some people get off on it."

"Look, you're good at the cyber thing, but my guy is better. He tracked you down. I told him I just wanted to communicate with you, I didn't ask him to find you. I kept my word on that. Trust your gut here, kid. I haven't lied to you."

"Why?"

"Why haven't I lied to you?"

"Yeah. Everyone else has. My whole life. Including that bastard you work for."

"I want to bring this to a close. I can't do that if you don't believe me."

"Why not just force me to—"

"I don't do that kind of work," I said, repeating what I said earlier before she could finish.

She was quiet again. I did not like at all the way this was unfolding. She couldn't be more than twenty. I'd lay money and give odds that the personal anger that emanated from her had some basis in fact. If the kid was four or five.

"Can I ask you, how old are you?"

"Why?"

"I'm trying to understand you. It's just a question that popped into my head."

"I'm nineteen."

I nodded. I think I had the reason why I was working through Garrett's lawyers.

"Look, for what it is worth I'm sorry you've been hurt and that people have lied to you. But I won't. I could have had a dozen people here to follow you. I could have asked my guy to find out who you were, and

I didn't. Tell me what's going on and what you want and maybe I can make it happen."

She was quiet again. I was quiet. The waitress noticed half her food was gone and asked if she wanted the rest to go and for her to put the order in for the chicken nuggets and fries. She said yes to both. I sat and waited.

"I don't know," she said finally.

"Start by telling me what you want if you can't tell me who it's for."

"Just the money he owes," she said.

"Can you give me a hint at how much and what he owes it for."

"I was told it should be about seventy-five thousand dollars a year. I don't want to keep dealing with him. If he gave me a million I wouldn't ever come back."

"What does he get for his million?" I asked gently.

"Get? Nothing. He owes it."

"To who, Rain? To whom does he owe the money to?"

She shook her head. "He knows."

"Okay. That's a start."

Maddie brought the food to go. Rain went to pay her and she said it was okay it had been paid for. She looked at me. "You don't have to pay for the extra," she said.

"I didn't, Rain. Garrett did. I bill all expenses I incur and I got a retainer from him."

She looked down. "Okay," she finally said.

"This number I have for you, I imagine it's an app or something, will it work? I can call you and text you at this number? I will be able to reach you?"

"Yes. For the time being."

"Okay. Then let's talk about what I will and won't say to him and agree on that."

"Okay," she said and waited.

"Can I tell him I saw you?"

She nodded.

"Can I tell him the amount and why you feel he should pay it?"

She nodded.

"Then that is all I need for the moment other than you telling me you won't try anything involving physical harm."

"I won't."

"What will you do if he refuses?" I asked.

"I'll tell. I'll tell everyone about him and his friends."

"Okay."

"Okay," she agreed.

"And he will know what it is you'll tell?"

A sarcastic kind of snort there. "Goddamned right he will."

"Okay. Tell you what. You leave first and I'll wait ten minutes before I go."

"Okay."

"Rain, one more thing," I said. "If you feel this is a legit debt that Garrett owes you or whomever you represent, why are you demanding that Evy not run for reelection?"

"She shouldn't be where she is. She is evil."

"Rain, you could pretty much say that about every politician in both parties and the wannabe parties."

"No," she said. Her face was grave, taut. She looked like she was in physical pain. "No, she's evil. She talks about women being equal and society treating women so badly."

"They all do, Rain."

She stood there trying to put words to it. It made it harder on her to have to leave somethings out. I had been relatively certain that Jewel was Garrett's daughter, since the conversation began. I thought about asking or telling her I knew so that it might be easier and I rejected that idea. I also didn't want to focus just yet, on the growing certainty that my client was likely a predatory pedophile.

"Not her. She doesn't just say it and do nothing. She," Rain looked for the words. "She makes it worse. She helps people hurt women."

I couldn't think of anything to say so I just nodded.

And she took her bag and left.

When I left the Corolla was gone. Most of the other cars were still there. The black Camry passed as I got in my car. Shit, I hadn't thought about that. I texted Eddie Martin that I needed to hear from his as soon as he had what I needed, no matter what time it was. I went home and took care of the furry children and woke up when I got a text from a number I know I'd never be able to trace."

"Black Camry and several other cars rented in corporate account under Garrett Thompson."

"Son of a bitch," I said out loud.

12

I STOPPED in Jeff's office and he updated me. Wayne Costigan had called and had a new case for us. We had an inquiry about a personal protection job. Tom was sick, caught something from his kid and Jeff would be on call himself tonight.

"I don't sleep much anyway," my partner said.

"I can handle it if you want," I said.

"No, you got too much on your plate as it is, kid."

I nodded.

I updated him about the job for Garrett and told him about my shadows in their cars outside.

"We should do something about this," he said.

"We will, pal, but honestly in the meantime, Garrett is just spending more money. And we know he doesn't trust me and that means he likely did something he should not have."

"There is that," he said.

"I'd have normally figured things out by now, pal. Truth is I'm a little foggy sometimes."

He nodded.

"Nothing is in jeopardy. All is going well and you're doing much better than most. Physically, how is the rehab?"

"Pain is a lot less, strength almost back to where it was. Not ready to fly yet but I can leap over small buildings with a single bound," I said dryly.

"Good."

"I just can't look at her desk, or my couch or bed and not see her, Jeff."

He was quiet. "And you blame yourself."

"Yeah."

"She wouldn't."

"Yeah."

"If it was someone else you'd tell them it wasn't their fault."

"Yeah."

"She'd want you to be happy, son."

"I know."

"There's knowing and there is *knowing*," he said. "It will be easier in time."

"It can't get harder, papa Jeff," I said.

I went out to my car and decided I'd take a ride and clear my head. I hadn't eaten yet. I passed Shaffer's and couldn't bring myself to go in as I went there a few times with Mandy.

I ended up on Victory Boulevard, so named because of the Victory Parade given after the allied victory in World War One. It had been previously named the Richmond Turnpike and you still might see a horse drawn carriage at the time of the renaming. Truck and Danielle got lost as I sailed through a light and a car had gotten between us. I headed towards the West

Shore Expressway and turned down the street where the West Shore Inn was and parked in their lot. My tails were nowhere to be seen. They would probably make for the West Shore Expressway. I went to the edge of the parking lot and stood by the wall, leaning and looking at my phone and I saw both of their cars pass at Warp four.

I walked around to the front and got myself in and seated. They had a small Filet Mignon that was perfect for lunch, and I had a salad with it, baked potato, and a dark draft beer. I had grabbed the *New York Post* off the bar and took my time and read it through. Feeling a tad sluggish I had 3 cups of coffee after.

Every year my family had gone to the Fourth of July parade that was held there, in Travis. My grandfather had lived on Roswell Avenue right down the block. We'd watch the parade and then have the best hot dogs and hamburgers on the planet, on this tiny charcoal grill he had. He'd have a huge garden with corn and tomatoes, cucumbers, and most anything else you can think of. He even tried to grow watermelons once. I had asked him and he didn't want to disappoint his grandson. They only grew to about the size of baseballs and he explained to me about how certain things could be harder to grow because of variations in climate. He'd been gone a long time now. I hate change.

The place was empty except for me and when the waitress came I asked if she would mind it if I stayed a little longer. She looked around and said she was sure that even with the crowd the owner wouldn't mind. The place was usually packed but today was slow besides me and a funeral repost in the back room.

I waited a half hour, and surprise, surprise, two

people came in and I knew one of them. I met him years back on a job. He was a licensed PI in Brooklyn. Leonard something or other. They must have back-tracked and looked in the parking lot. Not bad. Of course I had to fuck with them a little. My table was clear, and I signaled the waitress after she sat them at the other end. In low tones I told her I'd like something to go could she give me the menu again. She smiled and said she'd be happy to. She brought me the menu, and I looked quickly and ordered a plain hamburger and sweet potato fries to go. She brought the two refugees from the Sam Spade online course the menus and they ordered. They were trying really hard not to look at me. It worked out that I got my to go order first and I gave her two hundred dollars. Her eyes got wide.

"Thank you, hun. Consider it office rental. Food and service were great."

"Thank you so much."

I got up and headed toward the men's room. As I passed them I stopped. There was a young woman across from Leonard. She froze but he didn't.

"Jonathan!"

"Len, how are you? What brings you across the Gangplank?"

"Just lunch after a meeting. How are you?"

"All is well, pal." I used the bathroom and nodded again on the way back.

The waitress came back. "Hey, um, my back is kind of bad. Could I go out the back door. Does it lead into the parking lot?"

"Yes and yes," she said, smiling.

I was out and in my car and making the left on

Victory when they ran out toward their cars which were parked on the street but down the block. I smiled slightly and drove towards the expressway. I cut left down Roswell and passed my grandfather's old home. I took a left and then another left and drove slowly. They would probably go to the expressway and one would go north and the other south. With nothing else to do I took Travis Avenue to Richmond and went to Barnes and Noble.

"Ah, Jimmy, that was unkind," I said to myself despite laughing as I drove. They had probably left their food, too much money, and were likely very mentally and physically disheveled.

In the book store I ended up in the mystery section and walked out with a book called *The Grave Above The Grave*. As I got in my car I got a text from an odd number. 999-999-9999.

"All Garrett has to do is pay what he owes."

By eleven that night when I went to bed there had been no further response. I'd been a hit at home with the hamburger and sweet potato fries for Molly. Cory wanted to come by for breakfast and I told her the basement door would be open.

The next morning as I was working out I heard the door open and Cory came downstairs. She didn't say anything until I finished my set. It was supposed to be a medium day but I was feeling it so it was light instead.

She looked at the wall until I was done. She came over and kissed me, and I was suddenly much happier because she was there.

"Who is that?" she asked, pointing to a picture of a man squatting and obscene amount of weight.

"That is Rickey Dale Crane, who pound for pound is one of the strongest guys there has ever been. He is squatting 800 pounds and he weighs about 165 pounds. He is 44 years old there. I met him in 1996. We started corresponding. We talk online now. Good man."

"And these people?"

"Those are autographed pictures from Brooks Kubik and Bill Hinbern whom I also stay in touch with and train in the style that they advocate. I chat with both of them online also and once in a while Bill and I talk. That picture in the boxing ring is me with Rafael Williams a super middle weight and his trainer Pat Zagarino. Probably the best fighter I've ever met. I jumped in when his sparring partner missed a few sessions and helped Raff train for a fight he had in Mohegan Sun, in Connecticut with Vinny Pazienza."

"Oh wow. How was that?"

"Headaches and every bone in my body hurt for weeks. Raff is a world class athlete. He is way out of my league. I wore his over hand right like it was a hat. Also he took it easy on me."

"You guys that do that stuff...there is always this kind of bond between you, isn't there?"

"Often, yes."

"Did he win?"

"Against Pazienza?"

"Yes."

"No. But he should have. I thought so, and the crowd did, too. You weren't winning a fight against Paz in Connecticut if it wasn't by knockout."

"Oh."

"Boxing is a dirty game. It tends to use up and spit

out the fighters, and it's a hard as hell way to make a living," I said.

"Then why do they do it?"

"In the blood," I said. "Brain damage, pain, hard commitments, heartbreak. Dealing with crooks. Forget about the physical toll. Raff would get up at five am, run twelve miles. He'd work in a warehouse till three or four pm, then the gym. Training, bag work, sparring. Then sometimes weightlifting."

"Wow!"

"Yeah," I said. "Sooooooo, what's for breakfast?"

"It's a surprise," she said, kissing me and going upstairs with the bag she had left on the landing.

She busied herself in the kitchen and I went upstairs. I was in the shower when I heard the door open.

She opened the shower curtain and was standing there, a little shy, with nothing on but a smile. "So it turns out, I am the first course," she said, stepping in and sliding into my arms. "If you don't mind having dessert first."

"I like calorie free desserts," I said.

After, in the kitchen, she had made some kind of bake with potatoes, eggs, sausage, onions, and peppers. There were fresh rolls she had brought and some juice.

The we just talked for a while. It went back and forth from memories, to dreams she had. She'd ask me questions intermittently and we hung out most of the day. That afternoon I got a message from Tony to call him.

"I called the office. We are pulling double time tonight. Garrett said Todd would be leaving and unable to accompany him, that he had a special job tonight. Mean anything?"

"Yeah," I said. "And nothing good."

I got my computer up and running to get the information on the Corolla plate. DMV was down. I kept trying and it was evening when I got it. I got the address and went to the area.

13

THE NAME of the registrant and owner was Nathan Simmons. He lived in South Beach. He was a male, black, and in his seventies. My bet was he lived downstairs at 112 Thorsen St. His license included B on the address. Rain lived upstairs or was a neighbor. Garrett couldn't find her he figured I could and didn't trust me to know what was going on. My bet was that if I hadn't been here it would have been our last night working for him and Ms. Guevara. It was a safe bet Garrett was having me followed because he didn't trust me. Which mean he did something he didn't want me to find out about. And I probably lead them right to Rain.

When I turned the corner I noticed Todd getting out of his car. The numbers added up that he was at One Twelve. I lucked out and there was a parking space that I pulled into. It was about six houses away. I watched and saw the Toddster look around and walk up the steps to the house. Although the bushes of the house next door partially obscured it, I could see most of him and judging from the motion he made shortly after knocking on the door he threw his weight against it and shoved his way in. I was out of the car and moving.

This was going to happen and it had been the likely scenario from our first meeting. I knew what was coming. This was not a fight where there would be a lot of jabs. Anyone that tells you that old clichéd line "There are no rules in a street fight" likely hasn't had many. Of course there are rules. I'd had two hard fights with Tom Sullivan last year, who was actually a friend now. Well, he wasn't an enemy. Part of that was guys like us finding a way to test each other. This wasn't going to be that, for sure. Mark Stanton was rotting in the ground because my rule for that confrontation was he wasn't leaving that room alive. So there are rules when you fight for real, a lot of them. Mine, his, what the situation and geography called for, and what was needed in response to the changes. The rules were fluid and constantly being updated. Todd was vicious and cruel to an almost frightening degree. He was bigger and stronger and probably better. All that went through my mind in the seconds it took me to get to the house. As I got close I heard Todd shouting, a woman crying out, and a kid screaming and crying.

The door was open and he had Rain against the wall, hand around her throat as she struggled uselessly, and the child, about four, ran to her mother and Todd threw her across the room. I moved fast enough that his back was still to me as I drove a good shot into his kidney. He grunted and turned way too fucking fast for getting hit like that, and I drove my shoulder into him and knocked him ten feet away into the wall.

"Get the kid out of here!" I yelled at Rain who ran to the child.

He hit the wall hard enough to make the house shake. There was an old style glass window pane set in the wall that divided two of the rooms. It cracked. He roared. I don't mean his voice raised in anger. He spun around and saw me now, full on the first time. His adrenaline was in overdrive, and as we faced off he fucking roared at me. It was a primal sound infused with rage. Without even realizing it I answered in kind.

"Let's get to it, motherfucker," I roared back. As he and I moved and closed the gap, I yelled at her again, "Get the kid and get out of here!" at which point we met up each about half way.

My left hook never fails me. It's rare I had to throw more than that. He ducked under and deflected the right I threw after. I hooked him with a left to the body and landed against a wall of stone and he managed to move out of the way of the left uppercut that followed. I wasn't holding back in speed or power. He ducked under the right hook that followed. My left hook that followed that met only air. He drove a right hand at me and it was too late to block. He had timed it perfectly. I drove my face into it and took a good amount of the force out of it, although I'd have to say it didn't feel all that good. I ducked under his left hook and caught him hard on the bean with my right palm. His nose broke and his head rocked back, and it had all the effect of a butterfly kiss. He opened up on me and although I deflected, blocked, and moved away from most of it, I wondered if I'd be able to lift my arms after. Before I could set and move on him he barreled forward and opened up again. I caught most of it but my head rocked back and he paid me back for the broken nose in kind. I tasted the blood in the back of my throat from my nose.

The aforementioned happened in just a few seconds. I drove my right hand at him with my thumb positioned for his left eye. I was protecting the girl and her child and I was alone and fighting a psychopath who was bigger and stronger than me. Marquis de Queensbury was not a consideration. I had come close to pulling my gun, but I knew that would end up with him dead and me with a very uncertain future. Most people, especially those on juries, had no under-standing of violence or self-defense. Their most common frame of reference was television. He blocked the thumb and we circled and ended up slightly out of range. He rushed me and we ended up crashing into each other. My adrenaline was at a max. We struggled, he went for a takedown, and I got a hold of his finger and almost broke it. Had I been able to it would have ended things or ensured my win. The adrenaline was taking care of the injuries for the moment but that would change.

He twisted away and I hit his shoulders. He was at angle to me and we locked up. As we strained against each other I simultaneously felt something go in my left knee and my right ankle but I powered him away. When he tried to overwhelm me back I redirected him and he went stumbling toward the wall. He whipped around and we were just out of range.

"You are mine, old man," he snarled at me. "I'm walking out of here with your teeth and I'll drive your toothless mouth onto my dick when I'm done with you."

"Foreplay will get you nowhere Toddster," I replied, and more rage filled his face as shuffled in and I threw another left hook at him, followed by a right hook, both of which he blocked. We'd closed the gap and he drove his elbow into me and it landed above my right eye. I felt the skin split and it staggered me as my head rocked back. I heard white noise and blood shot out of my nose because of the impact, and being it was broken already it didn't tickle. He dropped low and caught me with a bunch of rapid shots to the body. I involuntarily lost my air and doubled over. He threw a really hard round house kick at my waist area that I got both arms on to block, and the force drove me back about two feet. It was definitely going to be fun lifting my arms later. Blood ran down from the cut above my right eye and blurred my vision. Blood went into the back of my throat and down my face from my nose. I stumbled back and created distance. He smiled.

We circled again. It's amazing even when you're in good shape how taxing just a few seconds of adrenaline-fueled fighting for your life affects you. I was still rehabbing from being shot and he was a pro fighter who could probably take a bout tomorrow. I hoped the fatigue didn't show because it wasn't showing on Todd. He threw a heavy jab at me which didn't land but the backfist he threw off it did. He'd used that to close the gap again. It gave me a cut inside of my mouth, and I tasted more blood. He used a front push kick that caught me to knock me back a few steps. He crouched, braced, and tensed, and I was suddenly thankful Tony had sent me that video. He went for the front take down and he got my knee driven into his chin and knocked him back.

He caught some of the knee on his chin and some he blocked, but that would have done a lot more damage to someone else. I heard the child cry out and looked in that direction, providing Todd with the opportunity to grab a small rubber or plastic planter with what was probably a tomato seedling and slam it on the side of my face. Damn he was fast. It knocked me back, and I was getting tired of him knocking me back. I let my hands and my head drop a little and he moved in, but I was waiting and this time I caught him with a good left hook. That knocked him back a little and he took most of it. Unlike the recent left that had landed on Romeo, Todd of the twenty-one-inch neck was affected but a good deal less. But he caught the full force. I moved in and caught him with my right elbow and this time the right thumb aimed for his eye landed but he had moved away from it. He growled and grunted and moved back, his hand involuntarily moving to his eye.

I did a stutter step in and my body language said I was committed but I ended up inches away from where I was supposed to be. I extended my hands as I did it and he came with the front push kick again. As I moved back he put his foot down and made his mistake. Arrogance and aggression. He had caught that guy on the video with a spinning back kick. It was hard, it was impressive, and no one with half a brain would ever give their back to someone in a real fight. Me leaning back and extending my arms a little encouraged it and that put his distance off. I shifted and moved in at a slight angle, and the kick, which had tremendous force behind it, sailed past me. I didn't need to do much other than redirect it and he went flying. I did help a little. As the kick went past me I turned towards my right and my left hand moved under his extended leg and I directed it upward and added to his considerable momentum and he hit the ground hard and uncontrolled.

And the motherfucker still rolled and got up. But he

had slowed. Despite that he threw a hard, fully committed left hook at me that I didn't have time to duck. The man was a beast. I got my elbow up and caught it on my forearm which smashed into my ear. He still came at me. I smashed my head into his face, his broken nose went flat, and he went into the wall this time through the glass he had cracked earlier. I grabbed his head and forced it along the edge. His face did a good job of clearing out the broken glass for whomever was going to replace that window. He screamed and the adrenaline spike from the pain enabled him to shove off but he had to use both hands. I stepped right and my go to left hook landed. He answered with a left hook of his own. Although there was a lot less behind it, you still wouldn't want to get hit with it.

I had turned back towards my right a little as I blocked and I drove a knife hand onto his clavicle with my right. My previous favourite sound had been the one this old girlfriend made when I kissed her. That was officially finally replaced twenty-five years later with the sound his clavicle breaking made. Another guttural yell and he fell back against the wall, his arm down and useless. Left hook again and his cheek bone disappeared as I caved in the side of his face and likely broke my hand. He went back against the wall and pawed at me with his right hand. There was another crunch as my right shoe connected with his shin. He cried out and collapsed. I dropped on the floor next to him and resisted the urge to keep pounding after I turned his lights out. And out he was. And I fell next to him. I woke up a few seconds later as Rain was shaking me.

"Jesus, kid," I groaned. "I told you to get the hell out of here."

"No, not without you."

She helped me to my feet and I looked down at Todd. His face was full of blood and swollen to twice its normal size. He was out but he wasn't going anywhere when he woke up. Aside from his face, his shirt and pants and the floor and the wall had been painted with our blood. I looked up and damned if there weren't spots on the ceiling. I looked down at myself and resolved that in the future, were there any chance of fisticuffs I would not wear a white shirt. I looked like a Jackson Pollock painting.

A guy I know, Marc MacYoung had coined the phrase "contempt will kill you." He meant that just because you have contemptuous feelings for your opposition, you having said feelings did not make them weak or ensure your victory. Todd would have done better if he understood that; he clearly thought he'd have no problem with me. That might have given me the edge that had me standing, well swaying. But damn, god damn, he was a beast. My hands shook a little and I wouldn't be surprised if there were fractures or even breaks.

Rain helped me into the kitchen and ran some water. The little girl had run in and attached herself to Rain's leg. I leaned against the counter. She transformed so quickly from not trusting me to nurse; if Todd hadn't used my head as a punching bag I'd have wondered why. Later, when I reflected, it hit me. I had told her I'd find a way to help her. She had sneered at that, because other people had said that to her a lot in her young life but no one followed through. She saw me firsthand go at it with Todd for her and her kid.

She gently wiped the blood off my face. She

grimaced. "Oh God your face. We have to get you to a hospital."

"No, I'm not letting anything happen to you. I made that mistake once, and it'll never happen again."

"What do you mean?" she asked, scared.

"I'll tell you another time," I said.

"Did someone die, is that why you're crying?"

"I'm cry—" I reached up and felt my face it was hard to tell because of the cuts and the bleeding and the swelling. I thought about Cory and then about Mandy.

"We need to get moving," I said. "They can send someone else."

I looked at Todd on the floor. He was out but he was breathing regularly. I looked around the apartment. It was, aside from where my battle with Todd had wrecked parts of it, neat and orderly. The walls were dark, and like many of the homes on Staten Island it was a solidly built house with charm and character.

"How long before can you gather some stuff up and get out of here?" I asked her. My voice was slurred because my face was swelling up.

"Ten minutes, why?"

"I'm putting you up someplace until we get this matter cleared up."

"But," she started.

"No time. You and your kid are in danger. I will figure out a way to help you. You can call the cops if you want, but in the big picture he didn't make a mark on you. He shoved Jewel across the room, but she's okay. Let me get you someplace safe and figure out what to do."

She nodded and went to gather their stuff. "If you

need more clothes or stuff I'll bring you back here," I called after her.

I opened my phone and scrolled through it. I called my friend Rhea. It had been a while since we had spoken but she had maybe the biggest heart of anyone I knew of.

"Hello?"

"Ree?"

"Jimmy? Are you okay?"

"Actually, boo, I have a problem. I have a young woman and her child that need help. Can you keep them over night for me? Until I can get them situated?"

"Yes," she said. "Come over."

No questions, no problem with it. Nothing about how late it was. She was that kind of person. She knew me well enough to know what it would take for me to ask that and why I'd be helping someone like that. I thanked her and hung up after telling her I'd be there soon.

The next call was to Garrett. It went to voicemail. I didn't leave one. I tried again and again it went to voicemail. I sent him a text message telling him it was urgent and that it would be in his best interest to get in touch with me. Rain came out with a suit case and a large duffle bag.

I used the camera on the phone and snapped some pics of the Toddster. He was stirring but I gave him a few minutes anyway. Never knocked down, never knocked out. I spit on him. I noticed something on the floor next to him. A white rock? Nope. A tooth. It was absolutely worth the pain of bending down to get it and putting it in my pocket.

"First time for everything, you rancid motherfucker," I snarled at him.

"Wow, your face looks bad," she said. "We really should go to the hospital."

"I wasn't winning any beauty pageants anyway, kid. We will take my car," I said. "Go out and wait for me."

She paused and stared at me. She looked at Todd and then back at me. I looked back and I knew why the fear was on her face.

"I'm not going to kill him," I said.

She searched my eyes for a minute and nodded. "Do me a favor, get me two glasses of cold water."

She went into the kitchen I heard the water run and she came out and gave them to me. "Okay, go wait by the car I don't want you to hear this. It's okay, go ahead." The kid had not left her side. She walked out carrying the suit case and came back and brought the duffel bag out.

I took one a sip and swished it around and hobbled over to the sink and spat out more blood than water, but it felt like the bleeding stopped. I drank one of the glasses. My breathing was slowing but my heart rate was still raging. I reached into the glass and took some of the water and washed it over my face. I walked over and poured the rest on the unconscious pile of refuse on the floor.

He groaned and made an effort to get up and failed miserably. I walked over and put my foot on his hand and ground it into the floor. I heard another crack and that made me happy.

"Pay attention, motherfucker," I snarled at him. "I'm going to let you live a while, but sooner or later I'm going to find you and end your pitiful life. But until I do, all you're going to think about is me owning you. You can tell that nouveau riche bag of pus you work for he's finished. And you remember, tough guy. When you can't walk for the next four months and you're in the fucking hospital, I did this. I'm going to come find you and do it again for fun. Then I'll let you heal again and kill you when I feel like it, at my leisure. Never knocked out, never knocked down? I can't wait to put these pics on the internet, Toddster. All those hours in the gym, getting needles in your ass, all that time practicing, and I put you down in less than a round."

He tried to look away. "You fucking look away from me, Toddlerooski, and I'll kill you right now."

His eyes met mine. He'd heard every word I said. The mighty warrior was vanquished. He couldn't hold my gaze for long but that was fine. He gagged and managed to turn his head as he threw up. That was fortunate for him because if he started choking on it, it wasn't my concern.

I couldn't do anything about my face but I knew his vision was blurred. Hell, mine was. But I gave him my back and strolled out like normal. It was hard as hell and I thought I was going to faint, but I walked like I was going to bed with a woman. I whistled "Beautiful Dreamer" which was a new experience in oral pain. I got out the door and went over to Rain.

One year, when I was young and stupid, well a little less stupid than I can be now, I had set some goals for myself. One of them was a super set of squats. Twenty straight reps with four hundred and five pounds. It took me six months to get it. I almost passed out when I was doing it and I threw up after. It was less effort to do that than it was to pick up that kid's suitcase and bring it to my car. She ran to her car and got the child seat out of the back and put it in my back seat.

I stopped by Todd's Jeep, and as he had left the door open, grabbed his briefcase and cell phone and a bunch of papers that were on the sun visor. That was another monumental experience in pain.

I met Rhea at the address she gave me. She was waiting outside on the porch. She came down to meet us, and cried out when she saw my face.

"Jimmy!"

"He won't go to the hospital," Rain said.

"Oh Jesus, Jimmy, you have to," Rhea said.

"I can't, sweetheart, I really can't. I need to take care of this. I got some injuries and it hurts, but I'm okay." I did know what was coming and I wasn't looking forward to it. One of the things that would get me through was knowing that no matter how bad I felt, Todd would be feeling worse. I had actually considered the hospital; the ribs had me worried, but the idea of having screwed up the shoulder surgery was what I was most afraid of. I took the occasional deep breath and although the pain level was in the stratosphere there was no watery feeling in my chest.

My phone started ringing. I took it out of my pocket. It was the G man, on his private number. I looked at them. Rhea was upset. I should have warned her.

"Sweetheart, really, it looks worse than it is, trust me. Please take them in. I need to get this call and I'll be right in." She nodded but I had convinced her of nothing. I became conscious again of my shirt when Rhea's eyes kept going to it. She'd look at my face and then my shirt. There was enough blood all over it that it looked like someone had thrown a beer mug full of it on me.

"It's okay, Rhea, I promise." I looked at Rain. "Trust her. I need to talk to you for a minute, so let her take the baby inside."

Rain nodded, went to the back door, and took the sleeping child out of the car seat. She walked over to Rhea and gently handed her off.

"We will sort it out and figure everything out tomorrow. You and the baby are safe now."

She nodded.

"I need to know something. Right now. It's very important. Is Garrett the baby's father?"

She nodded, and I grabbed the suitcase from her and told her to go inside. She did. The phone had stopped ringing. I leaned against the car and waited. I looked at Todd's phone. There was no screen lock. Idiot. Ten missed calls from Garrett. It was on silent. In a few minutes my phone rang again. The Big G.

"Garrett," I started cheerfully. "How are you? Are you at the Country Club? The Salon? Getting your nuts waxed? Well, I'm sorry, those raisins you have dangling under your cishood."

"Creed, what the hell is going on?"

"Well, Garrett, if you shut up and listen I'll update you." I could feel he wanted desperately to ask me "How dare you?" or "Who do you think you are talking to?" I could feel royal outrage at being addressed as such by a commoner. But he wanted answers more than to keep his servants in their proper place.

"Firstly, dear boy, do you have the address you sent Todd to?"

"Yes." I give him credit for that, the son of a bitch. No surprise, no reaction. No point in denying.

"He is there. He is in bad shape and needs a hospital. If I were you, I'd take him off the Island."

"Elaborate." I smiled. Thanks for that motherfucker. I dropped the manufactured good cheer.

"I walked in on him brutalizing a woman and throwing a 4-year-old child across the room. Your child, as a result of you raping Rain. You got that, you son of a bitch? He threw your kid across the fucking room. She's four in case your math is failing you. Do you understand me or do I need to dumb it down for you, motherfucker?"

Silence.

"He has a damaged right eye, a broken collar bone, probably a broken shin, and a few other things wrong with him. I did it by the way. Your resident bad ass, your paid for muscle, your teacher, your idol. I walked away with a couple of bruises, and I may go back and kill him if I keep thinking about it. I put him on his ass. You keep that phone on and we are going to talk about it, you and me and that moron socialist you own. Or actually let me put it to you this way. The moron socialist I own. And you, gare-bear. I own your fucking ass. Keep that fucking phone on and I'll call you and tell you when we are going to meet. If you make one more move on that girl or your kid, you motherfucker, I'm coming for you and it won't be to talk. Got it?"

No answer.

"GOT IT?"

"That's fine," he said calmly.

"Wise decision, Big G."

I hung up. I hated cell phones at a time like this. That really called for me to slam the receiver down.

I walked into Rhea's house with a resupply of rage

infused adrenaline and carried the duffle bag and suitcase. I left them in the entrance. I went through the porch into the living room and Rhea was there with Rain and the baby. I saw myself in the small mirror she had and affirmed why they were so upset. The baby was fast asleep on the couch and Rain sat with her. Rhea walked over to me. I looked at them.

"Okay, listen, I have to go. You're all safe. Rhea will take care of you. I'll be back tomorrow, I promise. And I promise it will all be okay."

"What about you?" Rain asked me.

"I'm fine, kid. Trust me, I'll take care of this for you."

"I do," she said. "No one has ever done anything like that for me or my child." Her voice broke a little. "I do. Please, at least see a doctor."

"Kid, trust me, I'm okay. I've been hurt worse than this and—"

"You wasn't gonna win any beauty pageants anyways," she said, mimicking me with an emphasis on the Nu Yawk accent.

"Dear girl, I do not speak in such a fashion," I said talking like Roger Moore. They all laughed. "I need to get you a lawyer, Rain. What's your last name?"

"Brady." I wondered if I had violated a rule getting and giving a beating to protect someone whose last name I hadn't known at the time. "Is Jewel the baby's legal name?"

"Hell no. You know what it was like in school with a name like "Rain?" It was torture. Her real name is Alice Brady. It says so on her birth certificate."

"Okay," I said and managed a smile. That hurt like hell and it was an effort to keep standing.

"I'll walk you out," Rhea said.

I turned to thank her and she hugged me, gently, conscious of my injuries. I pulled her close to me. I smelled her long black hair and she always had this faint scent of vanilla, rose and tangerine on her. I exhaled and relaxed and put my head on her neck. I think she told me she wore Perry Ellis 360. Whatever it was, when it mixed with her skin intoxicating didn't describe it well enough. She gently stroked my hair and pressed lightly against me. I suddenly had this vision or fantasy about me just laying my head in her lap and sleeping. Like I knew she would take care of me. I broke the embrace and managed a soft kiss. There was still worry on her face. She had these beautiful deep brown warm eyes.

"Jimmy?"

"Yeah, boo?"

"Be okay."

"Promise."

Before I got into the car, I turned to look at her again. She was tall, my height, long black hair moving in the breeze. Her face which brought to mind Helen of Troy was lined with worry. I didn't deserve people like her in my life. I had her, I had Cory. I'd had Mandy and I got her killed. She watched until I drove off and didn't go back into the house until I was driving. I needed to think. The office wasn't far. Everything hurt. As time passed the energy faded. I could make it to the office. As I gripped the steering wheel the right side of my hand decided that it had not been vocal enough and the searing pain made me realize I probably fractured something breaking his clavicle. Jesus Christ, six months still not fully recovered from being shot. I need a drink. And some pills.

PART III

My love is in league with the freeway
Its passion will rise as the cities fly by
And the taillights dissolve in the coming of
    night
And the questions and thousands take flight
My love is miles in awaiting
The eyes that just stare and the glance at the
    clock
In the secret that burns and the pain that
    won't stop
And it's fueled with the years
My love is exceeding the limit
Red eyed and fevered with the hum of the
    miles
Distance and longing, my thoughts do collide
Should I rest for a while at the side?
Your love is cradled in knowing

Eyes in the mirror still expecting they'll come
Sensing too well when the journey is done
There is no turning back, on the run.

"Big Log"
Robert Plant

14

IF YOU WERE WATCHING me as I tried to get into the back door of my office, you'd have thought I was drunk, or breaking in. I was unsteady on my feet, and at one point, I leaned my head up against the door. It was metal and it was cold and it felt good. I must have scratched the hell out of the door as I missed the keyhole at least a dozen times.

Eventually I got the key in, entered the wrong number in the alarm box enough times that after I finally got it right, the phone rang.

"Hi, code is Burke. I'm sorry, I'm tired," I told the girl verifying who I was. My voice was slow and slurred because my mouth was swollen and not because of booze. I stumbled into my office without locking the back door.

Squinting when I flicked the light switch on didn't make my face feel any better. I looked at myself in the mirror over the bar. There was not, I think, one square inch of my body that wasn't in pain. My mouth was swollen, my left eye almost closed, and there was a nice cut over my right eye. Painful as it was, I felt my shoulder, the one where I had the surgery after I was shot. It didn't feel like I had screwed up the repair. I opened the little fridge and got the ice pack I kept in the freezer. I grabbed the Jamieson bottle and sat behind my desk. No, I dropped into the chair. Part voluntarily and partly because my legs gave out. I might have a concussion, too. I opened the desk drawer. There was oxycodone, aspirin, some muscle relaxants, and Advil. I got the bottles of oxy and the muscle relaxant—flexorsomething or other—open and took two of each and four aspirin. When I dropped the bottles back into the drawer all the pills fell out and made a really pretty pattern. I took a deep swallow, and the fucking burn from the cut in my mouth coming into contact with the whiskey nearly took my breath. Sorry, it called for the vulgarity.

"Work through the pain, Jimmy Boy," I said to myself. I swallowed some more; I'm guessing the equivalent of two double shots.

Okay, let's not kill ourselves, I thought.

"Why the fuck not?" I answered aloud.

I took another pull but it was just a sip. I swished it around felt the burn intensify. I put the bottle on the desk and it fell over. It didn't matter, there was only about a teaspoon left. Time to head to the pharmacy.

Everything hurt. I looked at my knuckles, took a second to focus on them. There was a cut on my left hand, and both hands were bruised and swollen. That took a lot. I wondered if he was dead. Probably not, but I didn't care. That'd be something, though. I'd have killed two guys with my bare hands. My ribs vociferously protested when I leaned back in the chair. I felt them. I didn't think they were broken but who the hell knows?

Sleep started to force its way in, the adrenaline gone. I was exhausted. Leaning back had been a mistake and it turns out so was putting my head on the desk. I pushed back a little, found the wall and a position sort of leaning back, but not as far, and closed my eyes, pressing the cold pack against my face. Holding it there till the wall clock said fifteen minutes had passed, while fighting off sleep was perhaps the greatest feat of will power I had ever accomplished. I thought about Mandy and then Cory. And then Rain. Then Rhea. Rain's kid. My eyes welled up and some tears flowed but not a lot. At some point I dropped the cold pack and fell asleep.

I don't know how much time had passed; it had been well after midnight when I had gotten to the office. I was still sleeping when I heard my name being called from a great distance. As it got closer I began to wake up.

I saw Al McLaughlin, an attorney who rented several rooms upstairs with his partner Jim and an associate. Standing next to him was NYPD Deputy Chief Mike Mariano.

"You okay, Jimmy?" the chief asked.

They both looked concerned.

"You should see the other guy," I said.

"How about a coffee?" Al asked me.

"You a waitress or a nurse maid?" I said with a chuckle.

"You look like you could use both," Mariano said. Al wasn't smiling.

"I'd love coffee, Al," I said. "Guys, it looks worse than

it feels." Al left the room. I felt the pain but not as bad. The pills were still working.

"You want to talk about it, Jimmy?"

"In the worst way, Chief, but I can't. I'm working for someone. I'm under the attorney client privilege. I had this altercation with someone on the same side, and I can't talk about it without divulging what I'm obligated not to. If you give me a few minutes to clear my head, I will tell you what I think I can legally."

Mike's face was expressionless. He sat in one of the client chairs. Al came in and put the coffee on my desk. He looked at me carefully. I looked back. We'd been friends about 20 years and I knew him and his wife Donna and their two girls, Rachel and Victoria. We were usually busting each other's chops, so this was unusual.

"I'm okay, pal. I had worse."

"Okay, I'm heading to court. Take care, Chief," he said to Mike.

"You do the same, Al." I opened the desk drawer and took two more aspirin, another pain pill, and another muscle relaxant and downed them with coffee.

"Is there anything you can tell me?"

"Jesus I wish I could, Chief, believe me. I'm hurting, which is obvious. Every breath is a new experience in pain. But inside I feel worse. Like I have been drinking dishwater or I ate a bowl of grease."

"I'm guessing then your client is involved in something you wouldn't normally approve of?"

"Chief, that is the fucking understatement of the year."

He nodded. "You're a decent guy, Jimmy. I mean that. They had to sucker you in I'm guessing."

"No way to know what it was, Chief, until after I signed on."

I reached into my pocket and I pulled out Todd's tooth and dropped it on the desk. Mike's eyebrows raised. "Oh shit," he said. "You gave as good as you got."

"I gave better, Chief. He was good. I also tagged him first. But he was good. At one point he hit me with a planter so that evened things up. But to be fair, I hit him from behind because he tossed a little kid across the room and had her mother by the throat."

"Okay, that's good. At least it was self-defense."

"It was, and, it was defense of others."

"Any other damage?"

"Yeah. His left collar bone is broken and maybe his shin. Fucking moron tried a spinning back kick on me. He hit the ground real hard, uncontrolled, but he was up. There will be some bruises and problems because of that. And the right eye. Not ruined I don't think, but damaged."

"Oh shit."

"And his face came into contact with a jagged broken window pane, so there will be some cuts."

"Oh shit."

"Yeah." We were quiet a minute.

"I need to let my dog out," I said.

"How about I give you a ride?"

"Can I play with the siren?"

Mike got me in the door and I asked if he wanted coffee, and he replied yes. I put the Keurig on. I'd let Molly out when we got in. Mike offered to help but I told him I felt okay. The pills and the coffee had hit and I did feel much better. The cut over my right eye probably could have used a couple of stiches but it wouldn't be too bad. I still couldn't see well out of my left eye and the swelling was pretty bad. The ribs were probably just bruised.

"I will consult with an attorney and see exactly what I can tell you, Chief, if I can, and I promise I will give you what I can."

"What if this guy shows up at a hospital or presses charges?"

"With the kind of money involved here, I'm guessing he won't. He will have to go to the hospital. He'll say he fell. He won't go on the island, I'm betting."

The Chief nodded. I got up and got the homemade dogfood out of the microwave and let Molly in. I put it in her bowl. I thought about the fight last night.

"On the off chance I killed him I guess I could tell you what happened last night."

"Oh, shit," Mike said. "Give me something, just in case."

I nodded. "We were looking for the same person. A young girl. He was hurting her, I got him off her, he hit me in the side of the face with a small planter at one point. She had been doing something with seedlings. Tomato plants, I think."

"And you were both working for the same person?"

"Yeah."

"And you can't tell me what the work was."

"Yeah."

"Shit."

"Yeah. It's not that I don't trust you, Chief. One, I don't want to compromise you. Two, it's like giving my word."

"I understand, Jimmy. I believe in due process myself and attorney client privilege is part of that."

"Thank you," I said. "He is my height, he's got twenty pounds on me, and he's MMA trained. He got banned for hurting people," I said with a chuckle.

"Too warm and fuzzy for them?"

"Apparently."

"What else can you share?"

"I went to that address to question the girl. She's nineteen. She has a kid that is four. She calls her Jewel but that is a nickname. I was alone with him. He's bigger, stronger—truth is, Chief, he's the better fighter, I just been around a little longer. I'll tell you this, if it was while I was rehabbing my shoulder, I'd have shot him."

"You'd have been justified. You might have gotten away with it now."

"You have enough work as it is, Chief," I said with a chuckle.

"I was stopping by to ask how you were feeling, which I guess is a moot point."

"Turns out, Chief, I pushed it all aside I guess."

"What do you mean, Jimmy?"

"I focused on killing Stanton and not on Mandy dying. Or that even though I shouldn't feel this way, that I got her killed."

He was quiet.

"If I had just kept my gun on, paid more attention, I don't know. She should be alive, Chief. I got her killed."

"Jimmy, Stanton killed her, no one else. You helped break the whole thing open, them murdering your friend, Stanton's operation. You can't take responsibility for her dying."

"But I should have known better, Chief, I should have," I said and trailed off.

I must have fallen asleep again. When I woke up he

was gone. He had locked the door on his way out. Molly sat on the couch next to me and the cat had graced me with his presence by being in the same room.

I opened my phone and saw there were messages from Cory, Rhea, and one of my brothers. Jeff had apparently spoken with Mariano and he let me know he was around if I needed him. I responded.

Rain needed a lawyer. A good one. One to handle a lot of different things for her. Although I knew a number of people that could help her, one name popped into my mind. I had spoken to him once before. I scrolled down and found his number. I left the phone on the couch and got up. Getting up could hardly have been the biggest mistake I had made all year but it was top ten. I stumbled into the kitchen, found the pills I needed there, and opened the fridge. I was dehydrated, which of course would make the pain even worse. I resisted the urge for some more Jameson; it'd make me feel better but I was already dehydrated. I had quarts of coconut water and some power aid. I opted for the coconut water. I went back in, found the couch, and took the phone. I looked at the phone number and thought about it. I hit the dial button. Thirty seconds later he answered.

"Vachss."

"Andrew, Jimmy Creed here. I have a client I would like to refer to you, but prior to that I wanted to give you an overview so I wasn't wasting your time. May I?"

"Is confidentiality an issue?"

"Yes."

"Perhaps you wanted to run the situation past me, consulting with me as your attorney to let you know any possible liabilities."

"That is exactly right. I apologize, I misspoke. I had an altercation last night that is part of it. I may have a concussion and wasn't thinking properly."

"Okay, let's have it, Jimmy."

I told him the situation and got his input regarding attorney client privilege and it jibed with what I knew about privilege. I told him about Rain and what had happened. I gave him Rain's full name as well as the baby's.

"It sounds more to me like she was legally trying to collect child support and not blackmailing anyone. Give her this number and have her call me. If she speaks to someone else tell her to say I said I wanted to speak with her personally," he said.

"Can you help her?" I asked him.

"Yes."

"I remember reading about a suit against an agency that hired a repeat sex offender as a camp counselor, that's why I called. You should know, Andrew, the guy on the other side has a lot of coin, a lot. He'll have big firms backing him."

I didn't *hear* a snort, but it was there. I felt it over the phone line. He had made enemies of some heavyweights and he was always the one standing at the end of the fight. He had been the driving force in New York of closing what we called the incest loophole. It said, basically, if you raped a kid you were a monster and went to jail, but if you raped your own kid it was treated like adultery. Hard to believe, but then again New York, like most states, liberal bastion that it is, had animal cruelty laws before it was a crime to assault your own child. Hell, in 1904 the Bronx Zoo put an African Pygmy on display. Yeah, New York, you always were so busy

looking at the skyscrapers, or The Met or the Statute of
Liberty that you often failed to notice the litter on the
ground you were walking in. You could catch Patrick
Stewart in a great play and walk past homeless people
every five steps. You could eat at restaurants that you'd
have to take a mortgage out on to pay for and they
would throw food away while some kids didn't eat. The
other side, the Great American Family crowd, never
quite seemed to grasp predators have been growing
their own prey since there have been predators and
children.

It had been Andrew and the people that rallied
together against Sheldon Silver that closed it. Shelly
wanted the incest loophole kept. How the hell did that
take any interpretation? Yet he always got voted back in.
I had two celebratory shots of whiskey when he was
arrested and ended up in prison. Although in his
capacity as a law guardian, he would only work with the
child and neither parent. He did handle other types of
related cases. It needed to be someone like him to
handle what Garrett would be able to throw at the Rain.

We spoke a bit longer, I thanked him, and we hung
up. I called Rhea and she told me Rain and Jewel were
okay. They were both sleeping. I called Cory on her cell
and left a message. I got up, which was a little less
painful now, and got an icepack out of the freezer and
put it on the side of my face. Too little too late. My
phone rang; it was Cory and she was outside.

"I'm coming. Sweetheart, listen. I'll explain in two
seconds but I had an altercation last night. It's not as
bad as it looks, okay?"

That was a mistake, apparently, as well. I didn't want
her to see me like this without warning but apparently

that was upsetting also. She came in and sat down, and she looked at my face and started to cry. I held her and told her it was okay. She asked me what happened. This was something I was dreading. I was afraid she'd blame herself, because she got me the job. I was right.

"Oh my God, Todd did this?"

"I did much worse to him, sweetheart."

"Okay, tell me."

"Before I do, you have to understand—you remember that you signed that piece of paper that you were working with me?"

"Yes."

"We are working for Garrett's lawyer. We can't talk about this outside of Garrett and Evy. Not the police, not the newspapers, no one. I'd be liable for it and it would cause me a big problem in regard to future work."

"Why would you ever want to work for him again?"

"*All* my future work."

"Oh."

"So this has to be between us, okay?"

"Okay."

I told her the whole story. She listened and didn't interrupt for the entire time. Her eyes went wide a few times and her eyes filled more than once. When I was done, she slid in next to me, very gently. She put her arms around asking me in a whisper if she was hurting me. She held me and buried her face in my neck and wept softly.

"I can't believe she would be part of this," Cory said. "How could she?"

"People have justified much worse, baby girl."

"I'm so hurt. I feel so badly that I got you into this."

"You have nothing to feel badly about. This is what I

do for a living. We are going to help Rain and her daughter, and the Big G is going to pay for it."

"Can you help her?"

"Yes."

"What about this privilege thing?"

"I can't violate it. But I will fix things."

Despite the condition I was in I began to be conscious of the heat of her body pressed against me. I kissed her neck softly—a little spot that I had learned usually produced a shudder.

"Do you need anything? Do you want ice? Or pills or something? Are you hungry?"

"Well, funny you should mention it. I have read recently that intimacy releases pain killing endorphins, and although you'd have to do most of the work, four out of five doctors highly recommend it."

She giggled. "You want me? When you feel like this?"

"I'd want you if I was dead."

She looked at me, tears still flowing but she was smiling. She reached out and touched my face gently. She undid the top buttons of my shirt.

"Forget most of the work," she purred. "I'll do all of it."

15

I CALLED Garrett and told him I'd be meeting him and his two cronies at Evy's two nights hence at nine sharp. Haskins had to be in this somewhere. I called Tim Parlatore and he was free. I asked him if he could do a big favor for me and come by the house. He said he'd be there in an hour.

His eyebrows raised when I opened the door. In most situations the crew I ran with wise cracked. It's how you deal with what we see and many of them saw much worse than me. He didn't joke though and asked if I was okay. I introduced him to Cory and as we walked toward the living room. As we walked—well, as he walked and I hobbled—my right ankle gave a little and he moved much faster than a guy his size should and caught me.

"I'm okay, pal, thanks." I straightened up, and got myself seated. I told him what I could about the situation. He asked if this should be privileged I told him no need. He stared at me and I nodded. He nodded back.

"Keep an eye out for a call from the girl."

"I don't do family court, and Vachss is the best there is," he said.

"I believe she has...other problems. Shouldn't be a big thing for you with the friends you have," I said.

He nodded after a while. "Give her my number but tell her to text first."

I forced myself to stretch and did not consider anything else. I had just fought a fifteen rounder and I was taking some time off. Pills and a half hour shower. Hot as I could stand, cold as I could stand for fifteen minutes. I washed and did another fifteen minutes of hot and cold. The pills hit and the coffee got me to a few degrees of normal. Whenever I felt the pain I remembered how much more pain the Toddster was in. After I dressed, which, despite pills and shower took quite a while, I called Rhea.

"I took off a few days from work," she told me.

"You didn't have to," I began.

"They are no trouble. Rain is a sweetheart and Jewel is magical. I don't mind at all."

There it was. Despite Todd and the evil of his selfish actions, there was a child. Actually, although Rain was nineteen going on thirty, there were two children.

"I'm making breakfast. You should come eat with us," Rhea said.

I sat in her kitchen with some coffee and had adjusted myself to a position where I was comfortable and had a good view of her as she moved back and forth in the kitchen. She was wearing faded but form fitting blue jeans—painted on came to mind—and a light blue top. Her long black hair flowed back and forth down her back and she was barefoot. She moved gracefully, like a dancer. She was effortless sensuality.

"Are you familiar with the word callipygous?" I asked her.

"No," she said over her shoulder.

Rain and Jewel were in the living room watching SpongeBob. I knew the episode; it was called "Band Geeks." My niece liked it. It hit me then. Triton19. I shook my head. I'd seen a SpongeBob episode with my niece and the antagonist was Neptune's son, Triton. He wanted revenge. What he felt was his due. Talk about being disconnected. I suddenly felt old.

"Your ancestor, Athena, came up with the word. It infers beauty to a certain body part."

"That being?" she asked.

"The part I'm watching right now," I said. "It was initially used to describe the aesthetically pleasing rear area of female in sculpted form.

She grinned at me. "Did you just tell me I have a nice ass?"

"Nice, no. Beautiful would be more apropos."

We were quiet a minute. "I want to help them," she said to me. "Rain told me a little and she told me about what you did."

I nodded. "Why haven't you called the police?" she asked me.

"She'll have to do that," I said. "It's complicated."

"Are you in trouble, legally, I mean? That man was hurt pretty badly from Rain's description."

"Todd, the guy I left there, and I were working for the same person. Except I am actually working for his lawyer and I'm bound by attorney client privilege."

"But you could beat him up to help her?"

"That privilege does not obligate me to stand by and

watch him assault a young woman and her child," I said in answer to her query. "It's complicated."

She nodded. She called inside and Rain came in with Jewel and we all sat at the table. We had croissants, cheese, fruit, Greek yogurt that she had sweetened herself with honey, and she had made some scrambled eggs. Rhea suggested she take Jewel to the park around the corner that had a small playground and I could speak with Rain. Rain agreed. That was the thing about Rhea. Forget how beautiful she was, you knew exactly who you were dealing within five minutes of knowing her. Heart of gold, which has been on our lips in conversation since the fifteen hundreds and made an ever present part of our culture, conversation, and song since the Bard first put it on paper, was invented for women like her.

Apparently Rhea had made Rain welcome enough that she made me another cup of coffee when Rhea and the baby went to the playground.

I winced slightly as I reached for the coffee. "Are you okay," she asked me.

"Yes," I replied. "It looks worse than it feels."

"Your face is still swollen," she said. She looked down. "Thank you for what you did, for me, for my daughter."

"You're welcome, sweetheart."

"No one ever, no one has ever cared," she started.

"I'm sorry, sweetheart. I can't know what kind of pain you've had but I see what a great mom you are. I know you're a good person. I'm going to do what I can to help you."

She looked up. "Why?"

"Because," I said.

She stared at me. I smiled back and we both laughed. She looked into her coffee cup for a while.

"Rhea is so nice. She's been so good to us."

"She is an amazing woman."

"How come you and she," she started. "I'm sorry. I should mind my business."

I shook my head. "Timing was off," I said. "But you never know. Maybe I'll hit the lotto and things will work out."

"She told me about Mandy. I remember reading about you online."

I nodded.

"I'm sorry," she said.

"Thank you." I took a breath. "Look, I'm going to tell you what I can and then I want you to tell me everything about you and Garrett. Without getting overly technical, I was hired by his lawyer. You know the way a lawyer can't betray what he knows about a client or repeat what is said in confidence?"

She nodded.

"I'm bound by that. The son of a bitch did that so that if I found out I couldn't say anything. I was not, however, bound to allow that ape to brutalize you and your child. You can press charges against him and Garrett."

"If I do he'd have us killed."

"I won't allow that," I told her.

"But you can't—" she started.

"I promise you, I will not allow that."

She nodded.

"Now tell me how you met him and what happened, and let's see if we can figure a way to work this out."

"Okay, but I just don't understand, I'm sorry. You

saved us. I don't know what he would have done if you hadn't got there. But, no one..." She trailed off.

I nodded. "People don't normally help you."

"If I'm lucky. Sometimes they try to hurt me."

I swear to God were it not for the children I would pray every damned day for this planet to burn into a cinder. I searched for how to explain it to her. Had the thing not happened with Todd, she'd probably not believe me.

"Look, I don't want anything. Sometimes if you end up in a position to help someone and you can, you should. That's what I believe, kid. I know it doesn't sound right to you but some people are that way. I don't want anything from you.

"There's also the reason Garrett put me in a position where I am on the side of a predator. He's a child molester. I do criminal defense work but I wouldn't have taken this case."

"You defend people that rape kids?" she asked me.

"I do criminal defense work for people that are accused, not convicted, of crimes. Most of the time they did what they are accused of but not always. And in those instance the attorneys that hire me know that's all I'll do. I won't influence witnesses, I won't do extras, I won't pull strings. And I can always walk away if I feel there is a conflict."

She mulled it over. "I know it's a lot to think about but innocent until proven guilty has to be more than just words," I told her.

"But you're convinced he did it. You believe me."

"I knew it before you told me, I just needed you to confirm it." I said. "There is knowing and there is what a court requires as proof. Him sending Todd, your daughter's age, everything you told me. When I told him I knew he did not deny it. I'd never have taken this case if I had known all this." I paused. "And the son of a bitch had me followed and caused my word to you to be broken. I'd never have told them where you were."

"I understand," she said. She was quiet a bit before she spoke again.

"I was working on a school project. I lived with my mother and she spent most of her time drunk. Her boyfriend wouldn't leave me alone so I spent as much time out of the house as I could."

"Meaning he was?"

"He touched me. In the shower once. I screamed and my mother came in. He said he had just come in to the bathroom because he'd left his watch. I tried to tell her but she slapped me. She said I was coming onto him."

I took a deep breath.

"Garrett had a project to involve kids in politics. I worked there after school. He spent a lot of time with me and he kept telling me I was special. I feel so ashamed I believed that and I fell for it."

"Rain, you were a child. He is a predator. Did he know about your mother's boyfriend?"

"Yes."

"And he used that."

"Yes. I got pregnant and I don't know how he did it but somehow his lawyers made arrangements with my mother and he put me up in an apartment. I had to promise that I'd never tell anyone. He told me we couldn't be together then. I had a nanny and I had all the money I needed."

One predator stealing prey from another, I thought. "So what changed things?"

"After the baby we never had sex again. One night he introduced me to some guy he said was important. I spent most of the evening talking with this guy and he offered me what he said was an entry level position working for him. That night, after everyone left except for that man, he told me the man thought I was beautiful and wanted to be with me."

My heart rate quickened and I felt my blood pressure rise.

"I couldn't believe it. He loved me and he wanted me to fuck his friend. He actually told me the man was very important and that if I loved him I would do it," she said bitterly.

"What happened?"

"I got upset I started screaming and yelling at him. He apologized and got me something to drink. After that I woke up and his friend was on top of me, inside me, grunting like a pig."

I looked at the floor. "I'm sorry," I told her. "Do you remember who this man is?"

"Yeah. His name is Haskins."

"Son of a bitch. Congressman Haskins?"

She nodded. I fucking knew it.

"Was Evy in the picture?"

"Yes. She stayed over and she and Garrett slept in the same room. He told me he had to do it."

"So she knew? That Jewel was Garrett's daughter?"

"Yes."

"Did she ever participate in anything? I mean..."

"Not with me." She thought for a second. "But she did tell me once that we had to endure this so that we could free all women." She shook her head. "As young as I was I knew that she expected me to sacrifice myself for the world she wanted."

"It's always that way, kid. She thought it was a sacrifice for the greater good that you were raped. But she knew Jewel is Garrett's daughter?"

"Yeah."

"Does she know Haskins raped you?"

"Yes, she was there."

I shook my head.

"I told Garrett I wanted to call the police on Haskins and he told me I couldn't. He said that it would cause him a lot of problems and I would have to leave and that he could no longer take care of me. When I got upset he told me they would take Jewel away from me. I would be in foster care."

"What did you do then?"

"I decided I would save up some money and I would wait until I was eighteen and I would leave. I was able to save some. I could buy big ticket things at this discount place and I would return them and get cash. I even thought about staying because I never saw Haskins again."

"What made you leave?" I asked her.

"I heard him talking with someone on the phone. I think it was Haskins. He told him that he couldn't wait to see what Jewel looked like when she was older."

I didn't know what to say.

"I was ten months away from eighteen. I had met a woman who worked with victims of domestic violence. She told me how to get away without a trace, and I did. I had enough money to get a room in a decent hotel in another state. Once I was old enough and I knew they couldn't take Jewel, I contacted him. He told me if I told anyone about this he'd kill both of us. I took some classes and learned about computers and the internet. I read books and it came pretty easy. I knew we didn't have enough money to last for too long so I moved back here and I let him know he had to pay us. I just want what he would have to pay in child support. I can't beat him in court, not with his money. He could make us disappear, but we need money to live on. I'm alone, I have to raise my daughter, and I figured if I could make him realize it was easier to pay me off than the other stuff it would best for all of us, especially Jewel and me."

"So you started with the emails."

"Yeah. I learned how to hide and mislead him about where I was. I'd use a laptop and go to a library or like a Starbucks or just someplace with Wi-Fi I could get into and send him the emails."

I nodded. "I figured. He hired me knowing it was you. He wanted me to find you."

"Why? I mean why you?"

"You were smart. His people couldn't find you. Or, maybe he didn't know it was you?"

"How could he not?"

"Sweetheart, maybe you weren't the only one."

We both considered that a while. She asked me if I wanted more coffee and I replied water would be nice. She ran the tap water a while and filled a glass she put ice in. I was still a little dehydrated.

"Rain, did he do anything else illegal? That you know of?"

"Insider trading."

"Are you sure?"

"Positive. I wrote notes about it in case he wasn't cooperating."

"I'm afraid he may try to implicate you. You need a good lawyer," I said. She opened her mouth. I shook my head quickly. "Write this number down." I gave her Parlatore's number, and as an afterthought, Mariano's. "Speak to Tim about his financial information. It would likely involve tax fraud and you may get a fee out of the government that would not be insubstantial."

———

As I left, I called Mariano, told him what I could, and mentioned Parlatore. I called Parlatore also and told him. I had government contacts but so did they. I was almost home, and Mary from the office called and told me Jack Harmon had come by and left a message saying to please give him a call when I could. I did, and as we were both free, we decided to meet at the bar. It was the restaurant at The Hilton Garden Hotel, where I'd had lunch with Cory and punched out her ex.

He was having a glass of wine, and a Manhattan made with Southern Comfort and on the rocks sat waiting for me next to him. I pulled up the stool next to his. The restaurant was fairly crowded but the bar wasn't and there was no one on the far end of the bar except for him.

As usual I dropped keys, phone, wallet, and money clip on the bar. I preferred to remain unfettered and comfortable. I toasted his health and made the spirits fulfilled as they did what they were created to do. I felt that pleasant warmth spread and half the drink was gone.

"How's things, Sherlock?"

"They are as they are, Mencken. I miss her more than I imagined I could miss anyone."

He nodded. I sent the remaining spirits to follow in the path of the prior swallow. Jack signaled the barmaid, whose name was Sandy. I'd known her for many years and she was one of those people you really loved, and as soon as you saw her, you wondered why you didn't see her more often. We met at a gym when I was younger and being stupid (which is no surprise to anyone). I had warmed up by hitting their heavy bag, and when I noticed she was looking, I did as younger males and many older males do. I made a light lifting day a heavy one except I really needed the light day. It was she that ended up helping to pull the bar off my chest when I tried for too much weight. Talk about Karma. She also worked at Jimmy Maxx and held down a day job as well. She leaned over the bar and kissed me hello, and it was like seeing a friend I hadn't expected to.

"Hey, stranger. I figured it was you. No one orders SoCo Manhattans but you," she said as she put my second drink in front of me and refilled Harmon's wine glass.

"It makes me feel like Cary Grant or William Holden," I said. "And no one makes them as well as you do."

"Which makes me wonder why you ain't been around too often," she said, smiling.

"I am in error. I shall be around more often, dear lady."

"Better be," she said over her shoulder as she went toward people that had just sat at the bar.

"Is there anywhere we can go where you don't know someone, Jimmy?" Harmon said with a chuckle.

"I'm sure there must be."

"She's beautiful," he said.

"That she is."

We watched her and were silent a bit. He reached into his back pocket and took out his reporter's note pad. I had a small box at the office filled with them and they were getting harder to find.

"I did some checking into Garrett Thomas and his protégé."

"And the scuttlebutt is?"

"A lot of bits and pieces," he said as his eyes scanned over his notes. "Re-election is dubious but there is a lot and I mean A LOT of money being put in to keep her where she is."

"Would I be correct that she, pinnacle of equality and champion of the underdog, the working man, the planet, etcetera does whatever he tells her to?"

"You would be. But he doesn't really care about what it is she is about. Rumor is he owns Haskins also."

"I thought so," I said, nodding.

"Although they are mortal enemies on paper, they voted alike on two issues that he believes strongly in."

"What do we know about them, the office holders?"

"He is good in the sense that his staff is organized and on top of things. Her office is a mess. Good luck ever having someone from her office return a call."

"Sounds like that might be the difference between a career politician and someone elected to their first term," I said.

"Could be."

"How about the Garrett Evy romance?"

"Hard to say. They live together. They appear to be

together but a few people have the feeling it is only for appearances. There is no question he is the boss."

"Yeah. Observation backs that up."

"She actually has a degree in political science," Harmon said.

"And the military?"

"Nothing bad there, couple of medals, commendations, etcetera. But there's not much I can know about that, other than what's available to the press."

"I think I got that covered," I said.

"I don't need to ask, but she is a true believer?"

"Castro is doing a good job."

"Jesus, where is JFK when you need him?" I asked.

"And that is about that," he said. I gave him an envelope.

"What the hell?" he asked.

"I'm getting paid a lot of money and I can afford it."

"Nope, just a story if there is one. There is also some speculation by people I know about some of his investing. Rumor is insider trading."

I was quiet a minute. "Jack, I made a mistake. It turns out Garrett is my client and I can't use the information. If I could I'd have given it to Tim Parlatore or Chief Mariano, but I can't. I'm bound by attorney client privilege."

"Your face?"

"Someone else that was working for Garrett hurt a kid and I objected, but I still can't talk about it."

"Ok, Jimmy, but keep the envelope. I'll hang onto to the papers or throw them out or..." He trailed off.

I knew better than to argue with him about the envelope. We had another round of drinks and I sent Ray Gordon a text asking him if he could talk. His reply was "Fifteen," meaning he'd call in exactly fifteen minutes. I finished my drink, paid the bill, and left Sandy a large tip. I was in my car at thirteen. Ray had been a SEAL. Not one of the many people that claimed it but an actual SEAL. He spent fifteen years in the Gulf. I farmed out a lucrative maritime case to him a while back and we both did well. There were some people you knew for ten years but trusted them from the outset. There were some people you knew longer but would never trust. Ray was the former.

"Hey, Jimmy, what's up?" he asked when I answered my phone.

"I need to know what you can find out about Evangeline Gonzalez Smith."

Like most of the military people I knew he was somewhat conservative. "She's a communist."

I laughed. "I need more than that, pal."

"What else do you need?"

"Anything you can tell me. You're authorized twenty hours."

"My rate or my rate to you."

"Your rate to me, you piker," I said with a chuckle.

He snorted. "How soon?"

"ASAP."

"Done."

I had gotten home and taken care of the furry children when my phone rang. It was Ray Gordon.

"I spoke to several people that served with her." I had no idea how he got to them that fast. I wouldn't ask. "She served for appearances sake."

"Say what?" Which I reserved for genuine confusion.

"She hates this country. She would burn it down.

She wanted a political career and she knew that it would be good background. She even told someone that her political science professor suggested it."

"Like a paycheck cop," I said.

"Say what?" It was his turn.

"Mariano told me there were some cops who wore uniforms, collected their paychecks, and hated everything about cops. It was a job and nothing else as opposed to people who chose the profession to help people or stop bad guys or save kids etcetera."

"Good way of putting it."

"Yeah," I said.

"Jimmy, I can't charge you twenty hours even at a sub rate."

"You can on this, pal. Email the office the bill."

He thanked me and we hung up. It's a given that a politician, regardless of party, will tell you what you want to hear. It's a given that if it suited their being re-elected, most would change positions. They were sociopathic litmus paper for the most part. They turned color depending on what they were dipped into. But this, and what I was starting to learn about Thomas, was extreme, even for a politician.

16

A FEW DAYS LATER, after I let them sweat as long as I could, I sat across from The Big G, Evy, and Haskins. Haskins' face was bright red. I give him a year before a stroke. Everyone was quiet; except for the faint hum of the fluorescent fixtures there was nothing. I waited. Garrett tried to wait me out. It's hard to do that though, when you're trying to stare down a guy that put the baddest guy you know in the hospital. Staring is a game for people that are unsure of themselves. I didn't really bother with it. I made the exception. I had put effort into reducing the visible bruises. But you could still tell I had been in a hell of a fight.

Finally, Garrett looked away.

"Well?" I asked.

"I want to remind you that you work for my attorney and that you are bound by attorney client privilege."

"I don't need to be reminded of my obligations, Garrett."

"I can understand that you are upset. The job is concluded and you did what you were supposed to and

I have a bonus for you." He slid a check across the table. I pocketed it.

"So, just so I know I got it straight, G-man, let's go over things," I said.

"We don't need to," he started.

"We do," I said. Menace and anger seeped into that but my voice was still calm. "About five years ago you came across this girl at charity you contributed to. You found out before you raped her that she was fifteen. You were twenty-eight. Already a millionaire. At one point, you bought this solidified chunk of vomit and gave him enough money to win against the incumbent."

Haskins opened his mouth. I spoke before anything came out of it.

"Shut the fuck up, Haskins. If you say a word to me I will get up and drive your teeth out the back of your head."

Haskins said nothing.

"After you bought and paid for this walking pile of excrement, you tried to force the child you raped, who thought you loved her, to allow herself to be raped by said pile of excrement. Not knowing or caring that she was pregnant with your child. Then some years later, for the sake of power, you paid for this brainless, indoctrinated twit, to lie and win the new seat the Island got through redistricting. And said brainless, indoctrinated twit knows all of this but doesn't care. Just like Haskins. What is the sacrifice of another child for the greater good, right, Evy?"

Silence still. I waited a bit.

"Do you know what "Woke" is, Evy?"

No answer. "It's a state of awareness arrived at by people that are so fucking stupid they find evil and injustice everywhere except for in their own actions. And they don't care what they have to do to achieve the utopian ideal that they have been indoctrinated with, without ever having an independent thought or ever thinking to question it. And they will do anything, even employ the tactics of the enemy that they claim to hate, to achieve this." I resisted the urge to spit on her.

Again, quiet for about ten seconds. No refutation. To be fair that was because they knew I was a hair away from coming over the table.

The Big G cleared his throat. "That's about right, folks, isn't it?" I asked.

"Portrayed in the very harshest of terms," Garrett said. "And rife with prejudice. I had my first relationship with a woman when I was 12. I was more than ready for it. Children know what they want. Being minor attracted is a sexual orientation. Like heterosexuality or homosexuality."

"Pedophilia, the word you are looking for, Garrett, is in fact a sexual orientation. It is a vile unnatural orientation that was raped into a child. And the predatory pedophiles that act on it, like yourself, are the lowest form of life on this fucking planet. You sent that juiced up moron, whose brain couldn't jump start a Duracell, to the house of the child you raped, and when she wouldn't give in, he smacked her around and in the middle of it he threw a child, your child, across the room." I inhaled again. "It's a good thing you won't press charges, Garrett. She wasn't blackmailing you, she was trying to collect child support."

"Well, Jonathan, thank goodness you are working for my attorney."

I nodded. "You also had me followed. Probably

because you were afraid I'd find this out. And for that, Big G, you're going to pay extra—and I don't mean in coin. I haven't figured it out yet but you'll know when I do."

Silence covered the room for a few seconds and the faint noise from overhead lighting, which was at least fifty years old, hummed loud in that silence.

I smiled. "Yeah, I won't violate that, Garrett. Hard as it may be. But that doesn't mean I might not decide to kill you."

Silence again.

"By the way, Daddy Warbucks, you should know she retained Andrew Vachss to represent her. In this particular case, your fucking money won't help you. He can handle whatever you throw at him as far as attorneys go, and he will reduce you to ash. If you don't know about him have fun when you look him up on the net. If you make the mistake of trying to push him around, he has friends that make me look like a pushover. And, I promise you this, if you do try that with him, I will kill you. I will beat you to death over the course of several hours and enjoy every, mother fucking, second of it."

Silence still.

"And you," I said, looking at Haskins now. "How many kids have you raped, you fuck? What are you going to tell me? She was the first and last, it was a mistake?"

Haskins looked at me. He was a reptile. He was calm. "She enjoyed every second of it," he said.

"And you knew she was fifteen fucking years old?"

"Yes. And that's old for me, to be frank. You think they are kids? I've had "kids" as young as ten come onto me. And being a lawyer, Creed, I happen to know you can't implicate me without implicating your client. Everything he did I did. He supplied the girls."

I nodded. "That's right. I can't. But like I said, if you think that makes you safe from me, you are wrong."

"Really?" he said, amused.

I was out of the chair and leaning across the table, backhanding him. His head rocked back and he bled from his mouth. His eyes started to roll back. Pencil necks and flabby guts do not make for good shock absorbers. Garrett and Evy were careful not to move.

When his eyes cleared he stared at me. Angry I had the balls to strike one of my betters. "How dare you?"

"I dare a lot of things. I can do that any fucking time I want, Haskins." And I did it again, from the other side.

"Creed, that's enough."

"I decide if it's enough, Garrett. You lied to me and you enlisted my help, and you are a predator. You have no idea how much of a mistake that was."

"I can buy and sell you a million times. I can pay for an army, for lawyers. I can ruin you."

"And, if you need me to remind you, I can kill you," I said.

"Well then, I think it's best we all go our separate ways. That check is for two hundred and fifty thousand dollars. That will more than cover you. It is certified. You have been paid in full and far more than you deserve."

"I won't be putting you on my client list, Garrett. If you mention to people I worked for you, and you were happy or unhappy, expect to see me and it won't be to talk."

"That's fine," he said.

"As every second I remain here brings you three

closer to dying and me closer to throwing up, I'll leave you with this. If I were you two, I'd drop out of the race."

"Drop out," Garrett laughed. "I guarantee they will both win."

"Yeah," I said. "The man who would be king. Don't bet on it."

There was a ruckus coming from the reception area. As I stood and turned the door was kicked open. I saw people with bullet proof vests and hats and FBI stenciled in various places. They gave orders and we complied. Two men and a woman came in. The men both wore black suits and the woman a blue pants suit. They announced they were from the SEC. The FBI agents read us our rights. I was cuffed, an occurrence that was becoming alarmingly more common these days.

A few hours later I was in Federal Plaza, at the main field office of the FBI. Carmen Diaz walked in with one of the agents that had been at the campaign headquarters. I lucked out when they brought me to a car. I didn't get my picture taken but there were a lot of reporters, including Frank Donnelly. He saw me but turned his head.

"Hi, Jimmy," Carmen said.

"Hey, Car. Wow, it's good to see you."

"Yes, good to see you, too." She looked at the agent still in tack gear.

"Take his cuffs off, please." He did so wordlessly. "Your attorneys are on the way here," she said.

"Oh?"

"Yes."

Okay, that was interesting. I hadn't made any calls. Carmen's face, which was not something I minded looking at in the least, was soft and neutral. I had met her a few years ago. She ran the Innocent Images Unit, which was an elite unit that went after people who hurt children for pleasure and profit. I had given them a number of tips over the years.

I took a guess and said, "I can actually speak with you, Carmen, prior to him getting here."

"Okay."

"Tell me what you want to know."

"You were working for Garrett Thomas?"

"Yes."

"In what capacity?" she asked.

"That I can't say."

"Bullshit," said the agent. "PI's don't have privilege in this state."

"No we do not. However, I was working for his attorney and the attorney client privilege is extended to me."

"The SEC got a tip about illegal trading, insider trading, and it was indicated this meeting might be about that. They had the room wired, the whole place."

I nodded.

"We heard your conversation."

I nodded.

"Can you talk now?" the other agent asked.

"Agent, I'm sorry, your name is?"

"Bryce."

"Agent Bryce I cannot. I regret that."

"You assaulted someone that was working for him."

"Incorrect," I said.

"We heard you talking about it."

"I walked into a situation where someone that also worked for Thomas was assaulting a young woman, and he struck her child. I pushed him off and then he attacked me, at one point specifically hitting me with a plastic planter than had a tomato plant growing in it. I used the appropriate force to stop him from hurting me and them. I stopped when he stopped attacking me."

"Knocked out a tooth, broken collar bone, fractured shin, damage to the right eye, and about 50 stitches. What the fuck did you use? A cheese grater?"

"He was tough, he had a very high pain tolerance. I also," I said, smiling, "did a number on his knuckles with my face, in case you hadn't noticed. I probably have some fractured ribs, almost certainly got a concussion, left knee, right ankle, busted nose, and a few other things.

"You're still pretty," Joe Mure said as he walked into the room with Pat Brackley.

"Don't lie to him," Brackley said.

"Oh great, Laurel and Hardy for the defense," I said.

It was good to see them. And I almost fell over when Andrew Vachss walked in a few seconds behind them. He nodded to me. I gave him a slight bow.

"May we have a moment with our client, agents?" Brackley asked.

"Jesus Christ, the fucking New York Dream Team," Bryce said.

"Andrew?" I asked, puzzled.

The agents walked out and Vachss followed. He turned and looked at me, the slightest of smiles visible for an instant.

"I represent Rain and her daughter. I am here to inform them my clients corroborate your story and that you were defending them." His voice, which I had heard on television, the internet, and a few times on the phone, was the same. Low, strong, and Batman would envy it.

"Oh, and Jimmy," he said just before he was out the door. "You maybe want to work on ducking and slipping more." That was unkind of him because the way my ribs screamed at me for laughing was dehumanizing, but my laughter followed him.

"Okay, how did—" I started to inquire.

"Mike Mariano and Tim Parlatore got in touch. As Tim's friend at the SEC got the tip," Mure said, "he felt we should come."

"Yeah, this might be the current bout of blunt force trauma or the accumulated—"

"It's not like we had anything important to work on, like that homicide case I'm still waiting to hear from you on," Brackley said.

"And Vachss?"

"I'm guessing also Tim or Mariano," Brackley said.

"His clients are pressing charges against Todd Wilkins, Garrett Thomas, Haskins, and Ms. Che Guevara. They are also cooperating with Uncle, and as far as Wilkins and Haskins, I would imagine they will be served with papers for civil suits before they make bail," Mure said.

"I got a big chunk of change on this one, guys. I don't need any favors, I want bills." I paused. I had known them both so long and they had for so long been friends, I knew that had I been down and out they'd have never mentioned money. "Would you guys know, is Cory okay?"

"Yes. She's outside. Pretty, that one," Brackley said.

"Yeah, with a mug like that," Mure said. "It's surprising."

"You did just tell me I was still pretty, counselor," I said.

"I'm a lawyer...I lie a lot."

I smiled and remembered a line Vachss had written. "A real woman sees with her heart."

"So where do we stand?" I asked.

"They will release you, and we will cooperate wherever we can without you violating privilege. The others are going to have problems much bigger than you are," Brackley said.

"They have to be very careful because Thomas doesn't want to open the door to you violating privilege by him doing it first," Mure said.

A short while later Carmen came in and spoke with us and it went just like the attorneys said it would. She looked at me and smiled. I smiled back. Apparently *anything* I did, even the slightest motion like smiling, would be rewarded with pain for a while. I hurt myself worse when I thought of how much more pain the Toddster was in, but, totally worth it.

"This must be killing you, Jimmy, and I don't mean the injuries," she said to me.

"It is, dear lady, it is."

"We have more than enough on that recording, Jimmy," she said softly. "Haskins is already offering to trade a whole bunch of people, on both sides of the aisle."

"For every Denny Hastert there's a Eugene Gold," I said. She nodded and left.

We weren't there all that much longer. As my "Legal Team" had said it was going to go, it went. If I had been able to cooperate I'd have been there at least until nightfall. My gun was returned.

I passed Vachss speaking with a couple of people in the hall. I stopped and he looked at me. I put my hand on his shoulder and said thank you. His hand squeezed mine and he nodded.

"I'll take care of them, Jimmy," he said.

"That, counselor, is one of life's few rock solid guarantees."

He leaned in close and spoke softly, not quite a whisper but no one else heard. "There is some loss and some pain that you never get over. You can learn to live with it. Give it time. If love would die with death, this life would not be so hard. And you handled this situation right. We'll talk again."

I thanked him and went outside where Cory was waiting.

I didn't mind in the least the pain in various parts of me hurting when I caught Cory and hugged her. It was sunny and warm again for January. Mure and Brackley joined us shortly after. They had all parked at the same lot but Pat shook my hand and headed toward his office which wasn't far. Joe's car came first, and he shook hands and Cory kissed his cheek as she had Pat's. She drove me back to the office, at my request.

17

Cory sat talking with the girls in the reception area and Jeff and I went to my office.

"250 K?"

"Yeah."

"Are we keeping it?"

"Fucking A."

"I have the feeling you are going to put that to some good use. We are bucks up at the moment. Even with big bonuses we'll have forty left over with the initial retainer."

"I propose we put fifty in the business account and take a hundred each," I said.

"Are you planning on something with the extra hundred I'd want to know about?" he asked.

"Well, twenty-five aside for taxes. We are not having a bad year despite the current wreck running the country. I'll dump fifteen into retirement, maybe some gold and palladium, a little silver. I'm putting ten into the account I set up for Shane. I'm sending ten to Rain and her daughter. I'm sending twenty-five to The Legislative

Drafting Institute For Child Protection, that charity Vachss got rolling. The rest I have in mind for advertising."

"Advertising? Elaborate."

He laughed when I told him. "I'm taking 25 for taxes as well, 25 into the IRAs Susan and I have. Ivy needs a new car so take 35 and spread it among the charity, Rain, and the "advertising" campaign," he said.

Cory and I went back to the house and when we got in she went upstairs while I said hi to Molly and Reggie. The name popped into my head at that moment and the cat didn't seem to object.

Cory had come downstairs, turned on the hot tub outside, and took me by the hand and brought me to it. We sat in it for half hour. We went upstairs and showered together where she gently washed me, taking various lengths of time depending on what part she washed. I didn't mind that. We went to bed after and she insisted I lay back and she took charge, which I also did not mind in the least. After, I slept straight through to five A.M. She had stayed and slept gently next to me. I got up without waking her and went downstairs.

I called Leticia Remauro. She was a good friend and had also helped Jeff and I grow the company. She was politically well connected and owned several businesses, including a media/advertising agency called The Von Agency.

"Mr. Creed," she said. I could her the slight friendly bit of sarcasm in her voice and knew she was smiling. "Made it into the papers again I see."

"Ms. Remauro, I am in fact the local darling of the media, as you well know."

"Yes, and not too bad looking, although from that

picture your eye could use an icepack. Please tell me I'm not the one phone call you get."

I laughed. "No, I'm out. I want to give you twenty thousand dollars for a specific advertising campaign."

"Okay, what do you have in mind?"

I told her. "Well that won't win me any new friends. May I ask why?"

Leticia and I had spent a lot of time talking. I knew she cared about children. I read a book she wrote about overeating as a child because she was forced to and realized when I read it, it was also a chronicle of unintentional child abuse. She had run for office not long ago and was ready to take a sizable amount of public funding she'd have gotten and devote it to child protection. That was how I first got in touch with Vachss. I called and left a message asking for advice. Sadly, a political insider vaulted past her although she put up a good fight. In my mind kids lost out when she did. She and her daughter Jen had a podcast they did regularly, which I frequently listened to. I told her what I could.

"Jimmy, how sure are you about this? Haskins I mean?"

"It'll be in the paper soon."

"And that socialist wacko?" she asked, meaning Evy.

"Yeah, it'll be in the papers also." I paused. "I understand you may not want to get involved. It might get some people angry and—"

"If they did that, fuck them."

"I love it when your Italian side comes out," I said.

"I'm Italian on both sides," she said, laughing.

"Exactly, bella."

A week later, on the same day charges were announced by the D.A., thousands of dollars' worth of billboards with pictures of Evy and Haskins in cuffs went up all over the Island with the caption: "A picture is worth a thousand votes."

Whenever I would drive by one of the billboards, I would snicker and think that was some of the Big G's money being put to good use.

18

WHEN I GOT HOME I sat there and stared for an hour and literally thought of nothing. I danced around with sleep but it never took the lead. I sat there with my pain and although I was tired of it, it was going to stick around with me for a while. Getting up with the stiffness of an hour adhered to that pain was an experience I'd like to forget. I needed to think. I could also use a break from the pain that was ever present all over me. I did an internet search about the pain killer I was using. I was taking twenty milligrams, sometimes double. It wasn't doing much. I took a deep breath and was happy enough to smile that I felt no watery feeling in my lungs. Broken ribs could do bad things. And coughing wouldn't be much fun. The strongest legal dosage was only ten milligrams more. I spent a few minutes more than usual figuring out the strength of that pill vs the next one up the ladder. I took a hundred milligrams figuring that Todd, who was far worse off than me, had an IV and something much stronger. That didn't seem fair. I hadn't eaten for a while and I wanted it to last. I opened my mouth experimentally and both the cuts inside from my teeth and the soreness of my jaw let me know steak was not on the menu. I blended a banana, a pint of blueberries, some greens, a handful of almonds, and two containers of vanilla Greek yogurt with enough coconut water to make sure it wasn't thick. Everything liquefied. I got a big mug out of the cupboard and used three Keurig pods on four ounces and put three teaspoons of sugar and cream in it.

I took two Advil and two Tylenol as well and a fistful of whole food vitamins and something for joint pain I was experimenting with. I grabbed a couple of straws and sat at the kitchen table with dinner. After about twenty minutes the pills all hit and for the first time since beating on Todd's knuckles with my face, I felt decent. The thing about pain pills was there was no real sense of euphoria, at least not for me. It counteracted the pain. I did feel a little lightheaded, but that passed and the coffee helped. If I didn't have to think, I'd have had the Jamieson for tradition's sake.

Cory had gone but would be back later or in the morning depending on her dad. I was slightly euphoric which meant I had over medicated but not by much. I enjoyed not feeling the ever present throbbing ache head to toe from the battle with Todd.

"Fucking tomato can," I said to Molly. It felt like a classic Sci Fi movie was needed. I popped in my special edition Blu-ray of "Forbidden Planet." Although I faded in and out, I was awake for the confrontation with the Id monster. Molly looked at me as I snorted.

"Molly, dear girl, I'd like for you to meet Todd," I said. I thought that was just about the funniest thing I'd ever heard and laughed on and off about it for the rest of the movie.

"Morbius. Morbius!"

"What?"

"Something is approaching from the southwest. It is now quite close."

"That's just Todd, guys," I said to the screen and busted out laughing.

I found my way to bed. Tomorrow I would resume my role as Atlas. I took several bottles to bed with me and when I woke up at three-thirty because I had rolled over and every nerve ending I had screamed me into a waking state, I took a few more pills and went back to sleep.

19

"JESUS JIMMY, I was kidding about selling tickets," Bobby Z said.

A week later he and Frank were sitting in my client chairs same as they had when they came to see me not too long ago. They occupied the same chairs, except this time they both had coffee. Mary came in and she had that same sad look she'd had since she first saw me post-Todd.

"Umm, can I get you some coffee?" she asked. I never got tired of the brogue. I smiled. I never seemed to reach my coffee limit but I knew she'd feel better if she did something for me. I told her I'd love some. I eased myself into the chair, and although my face was placid and I didn't utter the groans and grunts, the effort warranted I was probably still a little pale and the sweat on my brow likely gave my condition away. I decided to wait on the pills in the drawer that were calling out to me, although I was an hour past due.

"How bad is it?" Frank asked.

"Looks worse than it feels," I said. If I said that once

more, to one more person. Frank had been around, so he knew. He looked at me a bit.

I exhaled. "Actually it hurts like a motherfucker. Fractured ribs, concussion. Did a good job on my kidneys. I was pissing blood yesterday. Broken nose isn't too bad. I'm going to have to have surgery to get the scar over my eye reduced or its going to open every time I sneeze. I have MRIs scheduled for left knee and right ankle because I don't know what side to limp on, and the rest of where the swelling is still hurts like it looks it does, and I swear to Christ there is not a square inch of my body that doesn't remind me about knocking heads with that son of a bitch at least once a minute. It's like a goddamned cacophony set on a one-minute timer. To be honest, as I told the Chief, some-times I don't mind the pain all that much because it's something to focus on other than the fact I got my fiancé killed."

They looked at each other and they were quiet. I offered nothing else. I said fuck it in my head and opened the drawer and got my pills out. Mary returned with my coffee and a glazed donut from upstairs. She knew they were my favourite. We all watched her leave and despite my condition and my heart break I offered silent thanks to whomever it was that had painted her jeans on.

I put the two pills in my mouth, broke them up with my teeth, and swallowed it with some coffee. I was down to where I didn't need more than two and had gotten by with one a few times.

"But," I said as I finished swallowing the coffee and drugs. "I also laugh my ass off every once I a while because I've been told he is likely going to be in the hospital for at least another three weeks. He was in critical condition for the first forty-eight hours."

"There is some speculation as to his future in the MMA," Bobby Z said. "He had to bow out of a fight he had next month."

"Broken shin gets you a titanium rod, allows you to walk on it while it's healing. Then it's like you have a reinforced tibia," I said.

"Oh great, you made him Wolverine," Frank said.

"Well, either he rats on his boss or maybe there is some jail time in his future," Bobby Z speculated.

We were quiet a bit, and I swallowed more coffee.

"Jimmy," Frank said softly, leaning forward. "We can all tell you all day what happened to Mandy wasn't your fault but until you believe it, it won't do any good."

"I don't think I will believe that, pal. I can't see it any other way. As a matter of fact, I'm with a beautiful woman right now and I love being with her and I feel guilty as hell at the same time."

"I want to tell you something," Frank started. "Years ago, a guy my family knew tried to force himself on my cousin. He was thirteen. I was young. I went ballistic. I caught the guy and gave him the beating of his life. He kept saying it was a mistake, the kid misunderstood him. I told him he had six weeks to sell his house and leave or he would catch a beating every day until he did and we'd go to the cops and get him charged. He sold the house. I never heard about him again until about ten years ago. He was arrested in Florida for raping some little boys where he lived, at a church he went to. Here it was all that time I thought I had done something good and it turns out if I had gotten him arrested maybe he wouldn't have gotten to those kids in Florida."

We were all quiet for a bit. Mary buzzed me on the intercom and asked if I wanted more coffee or if my guests did. She mentioned there were more donuts or did I want a sandwich. I smiled despite the grim conversation. I thanked her and told her we were okay when the guys shook their heads about more coffee or donuts.

After a while, Frank spoke again. "I want you to know, regardless of any good it would have done, if we had known anything about what Garrett or Haskins were doing to kids or that the female reincarnation of Che Guevara was standing by and letting it happen for the greater good, we would not have had anything to do with them other than turning them in."

"I have no doubt of that," I said.

"We just wanted to make sure you knew, Jimmy" Bobby Z chimed in.

"More than that," Frank said. "We want to make up for it."

"You didn't do anything you have to make up for, guys, but if you want to help and you have a few minutes, I can get you started."

I told them about Andrew Vachss and this organization he helped found called The Legislative Drafting Institute For Child Protection. In a life that had been dedicated to helping children and stopping predators, he felt it was his greatest contribution towards change. Essentially they would draft laws for politicians that were iron clad, with no loopholes for use by predators or their attorneys. And they would have ideas about laws that would make actual change. I called Vachss while they were there, got some info and his permission for them to contact him. That was an afternoon well spent.

It ended with them telling me that any client they backed would have to make realistic child protection a platform issue and commit to use the LDICP.

In the coming weeks I'd find I also suffered a torn meniscus and damaged my right Achilles tendon struggling with Todd. The scar on my forehead would need some time to heal and then Doc Testa could fix it. My insurance, which like most self-employed people I had to get through New York State, no longer had Dr. Shur or my physical therapist covered. Dr. Shur referred me to Doctor Riley on Staten Island and he went over the MRIs with me.

"Knee tear needs fixing but that is arthroscopic. Right Achilles tendon is in severe tendonitis caused by extreme hyperextension. Let's do the shoulder and give the ankle time to resolve itself. That recovery is a bitch, even though the tendon isn't torn."

The court cases dragged out a while. Vachss got child support for Rain and brought and had brought a suit against Garrett for raping her. He worked out some kind of deal and combined child support with the lawsuit and walked away with over fifteen million dollars. There was a clause that in return for not seeking child support he renounced all visitation rights. That was window dressing. He could seek visitation and she could still look for support as no one could legally sign away a child's right to support but it would be a deterrent for both. Garret had enough legal problems, and with his kind of money it made sense to get rid of the problem. Evy and Haskins were co-defendants and he would pursue them until he drew blood.

The prosecutor got an eight-year sentence for Garrett. Haskins was looking at heavy time and Evy got six months after pleading out and ratting on The Big G and Haskins. There was a bit of trouble for me after. I was walking outside the courthouse and a reporter for a progressive media outlet asked me if I persecuted minor attracted people. I hit him in the solar plexus hard enough that he had to sit down and turned blue. Another moron from a conservative outlet asked me if Rain had been with her family, might this whole thing have been avoided. That reporter was a female, and although I believed in equal rights, I couldn't bring myself to hit her. Although if she had been Evy, I might have made the exception. There was someone from the prosecution team nearby and she grabbed that reporter and informed her that Rain's "parents" basically sold her to Garrett and that charges were likely in their immediate future. It took Mariano a while to smooth things over with the reporter I hit.

With the new injuries I wouldn't fully recover until summer, but recover I did. Cory had gone to see Evy and asked how she could stand by and watch Garrett rape a child. The answer was what I told her to expect. Sacrifice for the cause. Because of Garrett, Evy would have been able to help people in Congress, although she did not do a damned thing while in Congress for two years other than spout rhetoric. She didn't make the life of a single person better. She accomplished nothing for the people in her district. I remember shaking my head when I read she still got a thousand votes as a write in candidate.

ACKNOWLEDGMENTS

Brian Drake, you the man.

Thanks James, Patience, Paul, Rich Prosch, and the crew at Rough Edges and Wolfpack. Thanks to Wayne D. Dundee, Owl Goingback, F. Paul Wilson, Mark Dawidziak, Tom Pluck, who published my first short story, D Dion, Stephen W. Browne, S. A. Bailey, and the late great Will Graham.

Thanks to all the MOMs. Special thanks to Mike Marino, who is actually cooler than the character based on him. Thanks to Ron Gorsline, who likewise is as cool if not cooler than Ray Gordon. And thanks, Papa Ostrie, who also cooler than the character based on him.

Thanks to Leticia Remauro and Patrick Kilpatrick for the help.

Thanks to James Lambert, Manus, The Big Kahuna, The real life Brackley, Mure, and Parlatore for the advice.

Thank you to Doc Testa for always being available for medical advice.

Also for Ruby Andrew and the LDICP.

Thanks, Charles, for picking out the poem. You're a gift to the world.

A LOOK AT BOOK THREE:
HARBINGERS

A thrill-packed ride filled with monstrous evil and good that prevails...

Jonathan Creed has labored for twenty-five years in a profession where he's seen the worst humanity has to offer. But his newest case reveals a depth of depravity he has yet to confront.

Creed's newest client, Hamilton Grant, has overcome horrendous child abuse at the hands of devil worshippers. Now, they want to claim him as their own. A dark and malevolent force, that perceives children as a commodity, will stop at nothing to gain control over Grant.

Thrust into a disgusting world where children are used for pleasure and profit—under the guise of worship—Creed must protect his client and put a stop to seemingly unstoppable monsters.

In a world full of good and evil, Jonathan Creed must descend into a terrifying darkness to neutralize a force as old as time itself.

AVAILABLE FEBRUARY 2023

ABOUT THE AUTHOR

You know that guy you picture when you read an old time PI novel? The one who stows a bottle of halfway decent whiskey in his bottom desk drawer? The one who sports a constant five o'clock shadow and—on occasion—abrasions on his face and knuckles that makes you wonder what the other guy looks like? Who has dark circles under his eyes because he hasn't slept more than a couple of hours since he pulled that impossible-to-solve case? He takes his work seriously but never himself? Well, that guy exists in the persona of John A. Curley–a martial arts trained, veteran Private Investigator, who is adept at tech and has a way with words, even if he does hunt and peck on the keyboard.

In his 35-year-career, Curley has worked locally, nationally and globally on wrongful death cases, divorce and custody cases, missing person cases, personal protection assignments and high-profile election fraud cases. He has logged thousands of hours on over 70 homicide cases—often with the defense relying heavily on the results of his investigations. Curley is perhaps the only investigator to warn his clients about Martin Frankel prior to his record setting fraud. He has currently assembled one of the most skilled and exceptional investigative teams in the country.

His passion for child protection led him to his friend and mentor, the sadly deceased Andrew Vachss—the foremost authority on Child Protection the world has known. He adopted Vachss' principles and advocates for our most vulnerable population. He has been responsible for helping to remove children from abusive situations while ensuring that adult predators are put away. He also advocates for stronger laws against child predators.

Curley is a consummate storyteller whose bold, real-life experiences provide a perfect basis for intriguing dynamic fiction. His writing reflects the stunning need for change in how the legal system approaches child protection and domestic violence. His short stories have graced several periodicals and in the collection, *Protectors 2: Heroes*.

He is currently writing the Jonathan Creed PI series. *Bonds* is the first installment—with two sequels coming soon. He is also lending his considerable skill on the collaborative novel, *Hard Stop*. Joining Curley's characters are the literary creations of Wayne D. Dundee, S. A. Bailey and Michael Black. The proceeds of this team effort go to the Legislative Drafting Institute for Child Protection in memory of Andrew Vachss.